KEEPER TURNED POACHER

Gerald Hammond titles available from Severn House Large Print

Cold in the Heads
The Dirty Dollar
Down the Garden Path
The Hitch
The Snatch

KEEPER TURNED POACHER

Gerald Hammond

Severn House Large Print
London & New York

This first large print edition published in Great Britain 2007 by
SEVERN HOUSE LARGE PRINT BOOKS LTD of
9-15 High Street, Sutton, Surrey, SM1 1DF.
First world regular print edition published 2006 by
Severn House Publishers, London and New York.
This first large print edition published in the USA 2007 by
SEVERN HOUSE PUBLISHERS INC., of
595 Madison Avenue, New York, NY 10022.

British Library Cataloguing in Publication Data

Hammond, Gerald, 1926-
Keeper turned poacher. - Large print ed.
1. Gamekeepers - Fiction 2. Country life - Fiction
3. Missing persons - Fiction 4. Romantic suspense novels
5. Large type books
I. Title
823.9'14[F]

ISBN-13: 978-0-7278-7649-2

Printed and bound in Great Britain by
MPG Books Ltd, Bodmin, Cornwall.

One

Tasker O'Neill let himself into his flat and checked. Through the open door to his living room he could see that there was a young woman sitting in the chair that belonged in front of his desk. 'What the hell?' he said.

The young woman, little more than a girl, did not move. As he saw on entering the room, she couldn't. Her forearms were attached to the arms of the chair and her ankles to the legs by silver Duck tape. He glanced quickly round the antiques, paintings and china. The room, pleasingly decorated in what had seemed at the time to be an appallingly expensive flock wallpaper, was as usual. Nothing, at first glance, seemed to be missing, which he found mildly insulting. 'What happened here?' he demanded.

The question, as he immediately realized, was a foolish one. She made no answer except for a loud humming sound, barely audible over the music coming from a large and top-of-the-range TV. Her lips were sealed with the same tape.

Tasker – nobody was quite sure how he came by that name and because he was both wealthy and short-tempered nobody liked to ask – had recognized her despite the face covering. She had, after all, been living as his mistress for several months. He walked past her, killed the TV and closed the curtains and then stood back and considered her. Her face, if he had been able to appreciate it without the distorting tape, was unblemished, symmetrical and would have been considered by many to be pretty, verging on beautiful. Her fair hair was natural. She had a very attractive figure, slim and firm-breasted, and she had been reduced, or had reduced herself, to a pair of decorative but minute panties. The humming sound increased in volume but he ignored it for the moment. She was unwillingly enacting several of his favourite fantasies and he hoped to savour them for years to come.

After several minutes of contemplation he blinked and roused himself. He returned to the oak door and made sure that the two security locks were properly fastened. This did not seem to be an occasion when interruptions would be welcomed. He took up a heavy stick and ranged once around the luxurious flat in case intruders were lurking, but the couple seemed to have it to themselves. In the spare bedroom that was nominally the girl's, a dress and some underwear had been dropped on the bed and beside it a complete change had been laid out.

He came back with a lightweight chair from the hallway and a miniature camera. When he had photographed her to his satisfaction he sat down facing her and picked at a corner of the tape over her mouth until he could pull it off. She squeaked at the discomfort as the tiny hairs were tweaked. 'Now,' he said, 'what the hell's going on?'

'Let me loose,' she said.

'Tell me.'

She looked at him without trying to hide her dislike. He was a stout man in middle age, losing his hair and acquiring instead the florid complexion and broken veins of dissipation. He had a strangely flattened nose with much-enlarged pores. Sometimes it seemed that he got extra pleasure from mastering somebody who hated him. She wondered if the secure and comfortable life was worth it. 'For God's sake,' she said, 'I've been here since just after lunch and it's not far off midnight. I'm desperate for a pee.'

He chuckled. 'Go ahead. The chair won't take much harm. And I want to know the details.'

If she took him at his word he would not be pleased and she would be completely at his mercy. She spoke quickly, almost gabbling, but arranging the story to save time by using the minimum of words. 'I had lunch with Sally James – that's the girl you made a pass at at the Hodges' party. I decided to walk back here through the park. That took me past the window of Craig and Grant – the big jewellers, you know?'

'I should do,' he said.

She decided not to mention that he might know the name but he had seldom been inside the place. He had not been the most generous of lovers. 'I was looking in the window when a man doing the same thing spoke to me. Perhaps I should have walked away, but he seemed a very gentlemanly man. He asked what I was looking at and I pointed to the little brooch with the heart-shaped ruby that I fancied. It was the cheapest thing in the window but my birthday's only a few days away and I was hoping—'

'Never mind that,' he snapped. 'Stick to

the point.'

She gritted her teeth. The central heating must have shut off and the falling temperature was not making her bladder control any easier. 'He said that I was the spitting image of his wife and he was thinking of buying a pair of earrings for her, they had a single big diamond each side, rather like the ones I had on, only mine were costume jewellery and these were real. But, he said, he wasn't sure that they would suit her. If I would try them on, model them, just for a few minutes, he said, he'd buy me the brooch. For a spur-of-the-moment story it was pretty damn good.'

'But your ears aren't pierced,' O'Neill said. 'Watch it! You're in no position to tell me lies.'

'I told him that but he said the others were clip-ons, the same as mine. And he was right, it turned out. I suppose that's why he chose them. Please, let me get up, just for a minute.'

'Get on with it.'

She let out a dry sob. 'Oh Jesus! I didn't see there could be any harm in it so we went inside. Mr Jenkins attended to us himself and there was an assistant standing by. The gentleman unclipped my earrings, the assistant brought the real ones out of the window and Mr Jenkins himself clipped them onto me. While he was thinking about it, the gentleman produced the money for the brooch and pinned the brooch on me.

'Then he said that he could really imagine his wife in them but he'd bring her in tomorrow and see what she thought herself. Just then another couple came in and the assistant attended to them. And then the phone rang and Mr Jenkins answered it. The gentleman, while thanking me very politely for my time, unclipped the earrings, put them down in their box and clipped mine back on. Then he took my arm and walked briskly out of the shop.

'Mr Jenkins said "Hello? Hello?" several times, as if there was nobody on the line. Then he slammed down the phone. I think he must have looked at the earrings. He came running after us. The gentleman punched him in the chest and darted round the corner. Mr Jenkins just fell down but I could see blood. When it sank in, I realized that he must have been stabbed, so I took off. Nobody was looking at me.

'I ducked round two corners and through the arcade and walked back here as quickly as I could without attracting attention. I was going to have a shower and change while I thought it over. But the door was only on the night-latch and they must have slipped it with a piece of plastic, because they pounced on me suddenly, two of them, before I realized that there was anybody there and they fixed me up like this. I suppose the other man was the one who waited outside the shop and made the call on a cellphone. And the gentleman took the earrings off my ears and I saw that they were the real ones, the ones with the price tag like a telephone number. There must have been some real clever sleight of hand, because I never realized until that moment that he'd swapped them over. He took back the brooch, too, which was a crummy trick, but he didn't touch anything else.'

'You must have been mad,' he said.

'I still am,' she said. 'For God's sake, let me go. I can't hold on much longer. I'm bursting.'

'Go ahead and burst,' he said. 'I've heard the words but I've never seen it happen. Why did you run for it? You hadn't done anything.'

Her face was screwed up with effort and her voice was pained. 'I have a record,' she said. 'A year ago, a man got rough with me. I hit him with a bottle. I didn't mean it to happen but the bottle broke and cut an artery.'

'Did he die?'

'No. But he came damn near it. I was charged with felonious assault and a whole lot else, but there were witnesses on my side. I was let off with two years' probation. Mr Jenkins died – it's been on the news a dozen times while I was stuck here. The staff at the jewellers' know who I am. If they make me out to be an accomplice of that man, how will that look? I'm still on probation. I'll have to run for it.'

'Yes,' he said slowly. 'I guess you will.'

He took out a little silver penknife and cut the tape securing her left hand. Then he sat back to watch while she freed herself.

Celia half scampered, half hobbled along the passage, leaving a trail of droplets behind her. While she had been sitting in that damned chair she had had time to think, but the future was so remote and unpredictable that it would have been difficult to fix her mind on any point beyond her present predicament. When she had got as far as the shower and the blessed warmth was coaxing away the stiffness and chill, she had the time and motive to give some thought to the shape of her life.

Celia Lightfoot's name had originally been Joan but she had soon left that behind as being too revealing of her plebeian origins. She had been born in the cottage in the Scottish Borders in which she had lived for her first seventeen years. Her father had begun as a gamekeeper, but the pay had been ludicrously small for a job entailing occasional confrontations with poachers, very little sleep and much odium when the birds declined to fly in the manner and direction which he was entitled to expect. Finding himself at liberty after answering an employer back once too often, he had decided that poaching would be more remunerative. It was a decision that he had never regretted. The price paid for pheasants was small, but they cost him nothing. Salmon, on the other hand, could be netted by a skilled man with a couple of strong sons on any dark night. They fetched a fortune at Billingsgate. And at any time of the year there was venison.

Celia's four older brothers held skilled jobs from time to time, but following and even exceeding the example of their sire they had also acquired a number of skills on which the law frowns. Locally, the family name became translated into Lightfingers. Inevitably, from being taken along as a reluctant lookout, decoy or distraction, she had learned many of the skills by observing rather than by doing. Other skills, such as fly-fishing and pigeon-shooting, she had acquired and even excelled at quite legally under their tutelage.

Her mother, however, was a fat and placid lady who, though not above pulling a vegetable or two out of a farmer's field when the family finances were at a low ebb, taught Celia – Joan as she was then – to respect other people's property. The unfortunate girl had grown up with respect for the property of others and yet with the skill to purloin it.

Rather than become rooted at home to be confused still further by divided ethics, as soon as she left school she had enrolled for training as a typist and later in secretarial skills. She had always been sure that life had more to offer her than as the daughter of the premier local poacher. During her schooldays she had been recognized as a gifted pupil but additionally she had set about devouring knowledge. She read omnivorously – there was little else to do of an evening – and devoted much thought to what she had read. She listened to the more serious channels on the radio, thereby also acquiring an accent that could pass for neutral.

Opportunities locally were limited so eventually she had left home altogether, severing her ties except for an occasional letter to her mother. Chance and a reply to an advertisement brought her to Edinburgh, where she worked first for a large industrial firm and then as a temp for an agency. She had rather hoped to save some money or at least to have some available for luxuries, but the margin between income and expenditure was always so small as to be negligible. She had hoped for a well-heeled boyfriend to bear the cost of dining and entertaining her, but the only suitors turned out to be even more broke than herself.

At least she remained honest. And she had never sold her favours. Not at least until the arrival of Tasker O'Neill; and even here only the strictest puritan could have called her a tart. She had encountered him first when he had asked the agency for a secretary who could be trusted to type, file and take messages. She had continued to undertake those duties and he had continued to pay her salary. Her other duties while under his protection had included being well dressed (at his expense) and paraded as a trophy. She was wined and dined extremely well and only occasionally required to share his bed. Even there, the duties were not onerous; age and dissipation were catching up with him. She lived well and her cost of living was virtually nil.

But it seemed that those days must be over. She might already have dallied for too long. Once the machinery for investigation slipped into gear, it would not take long to uncover her identity. Could they then freeze her bank account? Surely the unconvicted individual still had some rights. Not many, and certainly not as many as the criminal, but some.

She stopped the shower, tossed her shower cap into the basin and dried herself on a large bath sheet. Emerging into the passage, wrapped in another towel, she found that the door to what was nominally her room was stuck fast. Closer examination showed it to be locked.

The lights were still on in the sitting room but she found no sign of Tasker O'Neill except for a note in his sprawling hand on top of a cardboard carton. The note read:

You're right, you'll have to go. If they come here, I'm not going to lie for you. Your clothes are in this box. If you take anything else I'll prosecute you, which will turn you from a possibly innocent accomplice into a thief. Please be gone before I come back. Drop the latch.

So he intended to retain the few jewels he had bought for her. That might be considered fair enough by some. But the beautiful clothes? She supposed that they would fit her successor, because his taste in ladies was well established. But not a word about money. It occurred to her that she still had two weeks' salary outstanding, but there was no sign of a cheque. The box contained her office dress, some casual wear, one party frock, a tweed coat and an assortment of cheap underwear and shoes. At least he had got one of the several women who came in by day and cleaned and kept house to launder and iron the clothes, but there was no sign of stockings or tights. Apparently she was expected to carry her spare clothes in the cardboard carton.

While her superficial consciousness seethed at the cavalier treatment, a deeper part of her mind was sifting the facts into an orderly plan of action. She dressed rapidly from the box and a half-forgotten self began to emerge. He had even thought to put out her hairbrushes and her old handbag from the bedroom and she went back to the bathroom for toothbrush and toothpaste.

She was surrounded by valuables, but her mother's influence was still strong. If he were to prosecute her over ridiculous trifles she could call down scorn and derision on his head and he would know it. She helped herself to one good bath towel, some tinned food and a tin opener from the kitchen, a set of keys from the back of a desk drawer and a suitcase from the deep cupboard beside the flat door. She was tempted by a large suitcase with wheels but settled for a canvas case that could fold flat when empty. Hastily packing the case, she checked the contents of the handbag. Still no cheque, but at least he had put her purse into it and in her purse were her bank cards and a few pounds in cash. On top of the clothing she added four empty carrier bags from the kitchen.

Her library books were beside what had been her chair in the sitting room. She placed them centrally on the table where they could not be missed and she was ready. She glanced once round the home where she had been comfortable if not particularly happy, walked out and closed the door.

Two

It was a cool night, just at the time of year when spring thinks of becoming summer. She was glad of her tweed coat. Either of the furs languishing in the wardrobe back in the flat would have been warmer but totally unsuitable for the plan that was beginning to form, by a process of elimination, at the back of her mind. The shoes that she was left with might not be smart but they were at least comfortable.

She had come to know the centre of Edinburgh well. She walked to the bus station in St Andrews Square. This was still alive, but barely. The Left Luggage was firmly closed. She asked the sleepy clerk who seemed to be the only staff member present to look after her suitcase for her.

The clerk, it seemed, was not as sleepy as all that. He was a rough-looking man who had not shaved for some hours nor changed his shirt for days. 'What's it worth?' he asked.

It seemed to Celia that the time had arrived for being thrifty. Her money was limited and there was no saying when any more would be on offer. 'I don't have any money,' she said.

The clerk looked around and lowered his voice. 'Then gie's a feel o' yer bum,' he said.

'Not until I come back. *If* my case hasn't been touched.'

'Ye're on.'

At the nearest bank she approached the hole-in-the-wall and tried her bank card. As she hoped and expected, the police had not had time to identify her, track down her account and find somebody authorized to close off her access to her money. It was still not quite midnight. Drawing the daily maximum from the account and then waiting for midnight to pass before repeating the process nearly emptied her account but gave her a modest stake.

There was an all-night cafe within walking distance. She had visited it sometimes at the conclusion of a late date. She made her way there and sat drinking coffee in a discreet corner. While the proprietor's family swept around her, the traffic outside thinned to nothing and the clientele gradually changed from late lovers to the immoral detritus of the streets and then to the early shift workers, she puzzled again over her moves. She had some money, but a few days of hotels would exhaust it. To take a job, she would need cards and other identification. Casual work would still render her liable for tax and stamps. Her first thought was still the best – the keys that she had lifted from the desk.

When she judged that the time was ripe, she bought a hot dog as the cheapest sustaining breakfast and went out into the freshness of early morning. The cool of night was giving way to what might become a fine day. Her first destination, a shop catering to the downmarket motorcycle trade, had just opened and she bought the cheapest helmet on the market along with some coloured tapes, a length of wire and, as an inspired afterthought, a small switch.

Further along the street, activity was beginning at a large dealer in new and used motorcycles and scooters. She waited at a nearby bus stop. People came and went. At last a man, probably a member of staff, arrived, parked a motor scooter outside the shop and went inside. He had been so disobliging as to take the key with him, but Celia was prepared, with her small penknife ready to hand. She left the bus stop, and as soon as the man seemed to be settled, she wheeled the scooter round the nearest corner. It was a recent model and a not unattractive colour. A few seconds were enough for her to attach her wire, linking the battery terminal to the coil. Nobody paid any attention. One kick and the little engine was ticking over sweetly. She donned her new helmet, hiding her fair hair, and rode off. As she rode, her taut muscles unwound. She realized how tense she had been, but the dangerous part was now behind her.

Near the bus station, she found a dark alley where she stopped for a minute while, using bits of black tape and white, she tampered with the registration numbers. It would have been ironic to be stopped for riding a stolen scooter.

The clerk at the bus station handed over her suitcase. He was determined to claim his reward but she told him, in no uncertain terms, that if he came near her she would scream rape. She managed to position the case behind her ankles and to wobble round to the same alley. There, she divided her possessions between the four carrier bags and contrived to tie them on, two as panniers and two in lieu of a haversack, hung on her chest and back, with the canvas suitcase folded up under her feet. Then she was away. She filled up near the ring road. The period of damp, drizzly weather seemed to have gone past and the day was becoming one on which young men stopped thinking pure thoughts and girls walked with an extra wiggle. Spring, as already stated, was about to become summer.

Despite the Pentland Hills, Edinburgh is well provided with outlets to the south. It felt good to be departing Auld Reekie – a handsome city hosting government, law and finance but also crime, drugs and brutality. She left by a road headed in quite the wrong direction and worked her way cross-country by minor roads until she met the one she wanted. Then she was cruising south. A car could have done the journey in an hour, but the scooter carried a windscreen and her carrier bags to spoil its aerodynamics, added to which the first part of the route was generally uphill and then exposed to a head-wind as they crossed the Lammermuirs.

She turned off at last into a small town set in a valley below the main road. She topped up the scooter again, just to be safe, at a garage on the outskirts. There was a triangular parking area in the middle of the town among the shops. She squeezed the scooter into a huddle of motorbikes and other scooters where it would be least conspicuous. She stopped the engine, hiding her hands with her coat as she removed her hotwire. A headscarf, carefully secreted at the top of one of her carrier bags, was quickly substituted for the crash helmet. A man was watching her from the door of the gun shop, but being watched by men was part of her life.

Her first call was at the gun shop. This had a sign referring to guns and fishing tackle but seemed also to cater for every possible outdoor interest. She bought a large haversack. This not only accepted the two carrier bags off her person but also the shopping that she undertook at the small supermarket next door and at a nearby chemist. She treated herself to lunch at a small cafe, because it might be late before she could organize another meal – always assuming that her basic plan began to come to fruition.

When she set off again, she was navigating by a vague recollection of a route travelled, as a passenger, some months earlier. She left the town, travelling east, by way of a road that climbed on to undulating countryside.

The higher ground showed heather and the lower-lying land, being more sheltered, was mostly farmed.

While taking her shower she had racked her brains, trying to think of a suitable refuge. If she returned to her old home, not so many miles away, the police might already be on the doorstep. Her money would not last long even in a B&B and her earning capability had been aborted. She had been on the point of drying herself off before she realized that the answer was staring her in the face.

Tasker O'Neill had recently inherited a country cottage from an uncle who had kept it purely for his sporting breaks. The uncle, another O'Neill, had mistakenly believed that Tasker had a nostalgic longing for the cottage. Tasker, in fact, was not a rural animal and, during his schooldays, had hated every minute of being dragged protesting to spend his precious summer holidays at what he considered to be the back of beyond, far from any trace of civilization. But all had not been lost. A cousin, again an O'Neill, really did have fond memories of the cottage and wanted to buy it; but he was presently on contract in Peru and only when that contract expired in nearly another two years would he get the bonus that would facilitate the purchase. Tasker had been persuaded by a small premium to wait. The cottage was unoccupied. Celia, who in return for her keep, wage and the doubtful pleasure of Tasker's body was expected to conduct his correspondence for him and to keep track of his bills, knew that the electric night-storage heating was permanently on, to protect the fabric of the building. To this cottage belonged the keys that she had purloined from Tasker's desk.

The road carried very little traffic. Farmland gave way to patches of moor. Several tracks led off across the heather in roughly the remembered place and direction. After the lapse of time since she had visited the cottage with Tasker when he called on a visit of inspection, she found it difficult to choose the right one. She made one false cast and nearly ended up in a farmyard. Her second attempt was more hopeful. It was clear that this had been little used recently. Grass had seeded itself in the ruts. Brambles, always quick to grow, leaned across the deep ruts left by tractors. Tasker, she recalled, had been terrified for his exhaust and had taken to the heather in preference to the track, but Celia found that she could ride the central hump with little difficulty.

The track led her to a belt of mixed forestry some hundreds of yards deep. She rode on with birdsong and the scent of conifers all around her. When she emerged at the far end, her target was in sight. She was perched on the rim of a shallow bowl, partly occupied by a small loch of a dozen or so hectares. A feeder stream arrived from the far side, and the loch seemed to drain through a cleft in the ground to her left. While she looked, there was the splash of a feeding fish. To the right of the loch she could see the cottage. This seemed to have been made by the conversion of some older building of forgotten purpose, but the stout stone walls had a recent slated roof and she knew that the windows were double-glazed and plastic. In front of the cottage a dock led a few yards over the water, but the only boat was upturned on the bank nearby.

She rode down towards the cottage. Rabbits scattered and vanished at her approach. One observation concerned her. She would have expected the grass and weeds around the cottage to be knee-high, but for a long stone's throw around the cottage they were not much longer than the average lawn. She recalled payments to a nearby farmer for no specific service. If this were for cutting the grass, she would have to take care. She had no intention of attracting attention by being over-secretive, but nor did she intend to show herself more than necessary. With this in mind, she leaned over the handlebars and opened the cottage door, riding the scooter straight inside and killing the engine before it could fill the place with fumes. She had already checked that the gearbox did not leak. The engine itself, being two-stroke, held no oil.

On her previous visit, she had been tagging along while Tasker reminded himself of his legacy, so she had been largely incurious. She had looked inside, made the sort of comment that Tasker had seemed to expect and returned to the comfort of the car. Now she looked around with newly opened eyes. This was going to be home until any hue and cry had died down. Or, of course, until they caught her.

The cottage had been designed to make the most of the walls left from an older, rectangular building, possibly a small barn made redundant by changes in agricultural practice. The result was one generous multipurpose room, providing dining space, seating that included a bed-settee and a basic kitchen in a corner. The seating was grouped around a fireplace that held a few dry logs and some pinecones. Several ornaments adorned the mantelpiece but there was nothing of the least value and she suspected that any objects of interest or value had been removed.

Two doors in the back wall opened into a small bathroom with a shower, basin and toilet and into a bedroom with wardrobe space still occupied by clothes belonging, presumably, to the defunct Mr O'Neill. She was pleased to note that, though more broadly built, he had been no taller than she was and even his boots would be a tolerable fit given an extra pair of thick socks.

She would have pursued her researches further but her sleepless night was catching up with her. Sleep was rolling over her in waves. She lay down on the bed and was asleep on the instant.

She awoke, rather cold, in late afternoon. She had forgotten to switch on the immersion heater, so she used the electric shower to fill the basin for a wash. She wondered where the water supply came from and where the drainage went. But she had heard that what came out of a septic tank was perfectly drinkable and some things were better not thought about. Presumably someone who knew about these things had done something clever. All the same, she decided to boil the water before drinking it.

Continuing to poke into cupboards, she realized that there were a few rough towels but no blankets. However, she found a sleeping bag that seemed dry and smelled reasonably clean. Needs must.

The next task was to get some idea of the immediate environs. She donned a pair of stout brogues over extra socks and found them tolerably comfortable. Away from the cottage, grass and weeds had been allowed to riot, and with them wildflowers giving a delicate scattering of colour, but there were paths made by people or wildlife trodden through the jungle. She walked round the loch. Bracken took over the ground. Reflected in the water with a background of towering trees, the cottage made a scene that was almost chocolate-box. The sunlight brought out hidden colours – blue in the slates, russets and purples in the stonework and a hundred splashes and shades of colour among the greenery. Over all, the sky was very blue.

She penetrated outwards to look over the

surrounding land. The few visible dwellings were mostly some distance off but the ground undulated so that there were ample areas of dead ground in which houses could be invisible. Time would tell. To the north and east the heather continued to the horizon, but south and westward to Newton Lauder there was what looked like good mixed farmland. She could see cattle and also different shades of green, suggesting a variety of crops.

She returned to the cottage and made herself a meal from the supplies that she had brought, but these would not last forever. There was a gun safe in a cupboard beside the entrance door. Mr O'Neill's beneficiaries would have been inviting prosecution if they had left firearms in an unoccupied cottage. The gun safe was locked. It might only be being used as a secure repository for valuables, but she was curious. The keys were on the ring. She opened the gun safe and was gratified to find a good-quality air rifle and a supply of slugs. The air rifle would not legally be a firearm but at close range, up to about twenty yards, it would be quite capable of gathering a rabbit or pigeon. A glance out of the window showed that rabbits, made bold by a long period of being ignored, were sunning themselves on the grass. This should be easier than setting snares. She opened the door a crack and seated herself on a low chair with her elbows on her knees.

Her first shot missed but she saw the grass jump beyond the rabbit's ears. Lowering her aim, she killed three in succession, all head shots. That would do for the moment. The other rabbits seemed quite unperturbed by the sound of the shots, which anyway would mostly have been confined to the interior of the cottage. She went outside and waited until the dozens of surviving rabbits had retreated down their holes before picking up her modest bag. She gutted them into the loch where the extra nourishment might be appreciated by the resident trout.

Outside the cottage, at the gable, there was a meat-safe made from an old upright chill cabinet out of a shop. She hung her rabbits inside. The weather was turning warm and she would eat them soon.

Dusk was approaching and sleep was creeping up on her again. Already Edinburgh was receding in her memory and the cottage was beginning to seem like home.

Three

The cottage was equipped with electric lights, neatly shaded. She was quite sure that there was nobody near enough even to see the glow of a light, yet the idea of undressing with the light on and the windows black and uncovered seemed like an invitation to any passing pervert or rapist. She added *curtain material* to her shopping list, undressed in the dark, donned one of the shirts from the wardrobe as a substitute nightie and entered the sleeping bag.

Sleep arrived slowly. She invited it closer by trying to imagine the history of the cottage, its agricultural beginnings, its conversion into a sporting pied à terre and then ... She was sensitive to atmosphere and there was something welcoming, almost loving about the place. Had it been a love-nest? She was asleep before she arrived at any conclusion.

After sleeping away the middle of the

previous day, it was no wonder that she awoke with the dawn. She had already decided to devote the day to settling in along with all the mundane chores. But first she took down the trout rod from a row of hooks on the wall. There had been a fishing bag in the cupboard with the gun safe and it contained a fly-box with a useful selection hooked into the foam in the trays. She tied a cast with a bloody butcher on point and a lighter caddis on the single dropper and, wearing an old fishing hat borrowed again from the cottage's late owner, carried the set-up down to the dock. She would have liked to launch the dinghy but its planks had been drying out and she could see daylight between. The dock, of scaffolding poles and old railway sleepers, was not in a much better shape but it would do. The rod was well suited to her.

As with the rabbits, the trout had not been disturbed during the lifetime of many, so they did not associate the human silhouette with danger. A rise began with the first hatch and she soon had two brown trout, each of more than a pound. There was no point being greedy – the fish might become educated and suspicious. She returned to the cottage and stowed the fish in the small refrigerator, which had been switched on and cooling overnight.

The cottage was better equipped than many such bachelor haunts. There was, for instance, an electric shower as well as a good cooker and the fridge already referred to, but its amenities did not include a washing machine or a microwave. She did her small laundry by hand and hung it in one of the trees where she thought it was screened from casual view. A few minutes of logical thought enabled her to incorporate into the wiring of the scooter the small switch that she had brought with her so that she could at least start and stop the small engine without too obviously going through the motions of the thief.

There was a transistor radio. It suffered from a flat battery but in a kitchen drawer she had found a lead designed to connect the radio to the electric mains. She had music and news, contact with the outside world. But these, she admitted to herself, were merely devices to postpone the one action that was necessary but which she dreaded. Among her purchases the previous day had been a bottle of black hair dye. She stood for a few minutes before the only large mirror. Her fair hair had been a part of her for as long as she could remember. She considered it to be her most noticeable feature. Any description of her, broadcast or circulated, would begin with it. Now it must go.

She turned away quickly, looked out the bottle of black dye and read the instructions carefully. When the dread deed was done, she decided not to waste the warm breeze. She carried a chair outside, carefully scanning her surroundings for human figures, and protected the chair with paper towels. The radio was offering no talks of any interest. She had never been inclined to use music as more than a background, to be heard without actually listening. She had noticed a pile of magazines beside the gun safe. To pass the time, she fetched them.

These were a disappointment as reading matter. They proved to be largely photographic soft porn of the lingerie and bondage variety and did nothing for her except to give her a little food for thought while she waited for her hair to dry. She decided that if all else failed she could offer her services as a model. After all, she was not inexperienced. Glancing at the accompanying text, she realized that she could also write much more interesting and more credible accounts of how the young ladies came to be in their photogenic predicaments. Her own true story would make an excellent start if she could persuade Tasker O'Neill to part with copies of his photographs.

At this point in her deliberations she sensed that she was not alone. She looked up, startled, half expecting a policeman. A dog, a spaniel, was sitting a few yards away, looking at her in doubt. Its coat was matted and it was very muddy but its ribs still managed to show.

'Hullo,' she said. 'Who are you?' She snapped her fingers. She did not expect a reply but at least an approach would have been in order. But the dog, while seeming prepared for flight, also managed a small wag of the docked tail and sat tight, passing a pink tongue over its lips. Its eyes remained bright.

Celia knew dogs. Her father's cottage had seldom been without several. This dog – she could see now that she was a bitch – was hungry. Celia got up and put the kettle on. While it boiled, she looked in the cupboards. There were some biscuits, of a make that she rather disliked, and a cold boiled potato. The spaniel, she discovered, made bold by hunger, had followed her inside, holding out a paw but then withdrawing before she could take it. Hunger continued to overcome timidity. When she offered her largesse, the gifts were accepted, gently and politely, from her hand. Which was all very well, but the spaniel was still ravenous.

If Celia had a soft spot it was for dogs, spaniels especially. She could no more have turned away a hungry spaniel than kicked a kitten. She had intended a trout for her evening meal, but she was not at all sure how fish bones would agree with a dog. She had intended to dine on rabbit next day, but it seemed that her planned menus needed revision. She brought in one of her rabbits and prepared it. Taken raw, the rabbit might have transmitted tapeworm. Happily, there was a pressure cooker among the pans.

While the rabbit cooked, it seemed that they would have most of a half-hour to spare. 'You,' Celia said, 'are an exceptionally mucky pup.' But she said it kindly and the remark was greeted by a wag of the whole butt-end. She led the spaniel into the shower, protecting herself with a waxed coat from the hall cupboard, and kneeling alongside she used some of her own shampoo. As she washed, she was startled to feel how much the ribs stood proud. The spaniel stood still, accepting the attention but flinching momentarily. A careful examination, parting the hair, revealed bruises. At first glance these might have been the result of getting lost and living rough, but patient study showed a different pattern. Across the back were weals, as of blows from a stick or a chain lead. Lower on the body were more rounded bruises. If the bitch's owner was in the habit of kicking or whipping her, no wonder she had run away. To any other emotions were added anger and compassion.

After the third rinse, when the water was at last running clean, she led the spaniel outside, carrying the pressure cooker out with her to cool. She was not prepared to sacrifice a towel so she squeezed the water out and teased the soft fur in the warm breeze, finishing the job with her own brush and comb. It was now possible for them to look at each other. The spaniel was now seen to be a good-looking but emaciated springer bitch. Celia, seeing herself in a mirror while brushing out her hair, was surprised to see how well dark hair suited her.

'We make a handsome couple,' she said. The remark was rewarded with a couple of wags of the docked tail and a quick prance, but the spaniel was more interested in food. Celia found a plastic basin. The meat was now cool enough to handle and she separated about half the meat into the basin, added some biscuit and breadcrumbs and the cold potato and carried it outside. When she put the basin down, the spaniel hurled herself at it. Without pausing for breath, she gobbled what Celia was sure would have been a day's rations for a spaniel in ordinary circumstances, and sat, looking hopefully again.

Celia had intended to keep the other half of the rabbit's meat for her own dinner, but she was unable to resist those liquid eyes. She dished out the remainder of the meat. Whether cooked rabbit bones were permissible had become vague in her memory; she rather thought not. She disposed of them safely in the loch.

The spaniel was now looking distinctly portly. 'If you want to go home,' Celia told her, 'now might be a good time.' She waited anxiously. The suggestion had been made for a variety of reasons. The bruises might not have been inflicted by the real owner, who might now be pining for a beloved pet. Moreover, there had been no transfer of ownership. Also, the presence of a dependent spaniel might prove inconvenient and costly. But she hoped very much that cupboard love and a response to kindness might prevail.

The spaniel sat tight, her stump of tail brushing to and fro across the grass.

'I can't really blame you,' Celia said. It was becoming a relief to have another creature to talk to. The spaniel gave every sign of comprehension, although Celia knew that it was the kindness and acceptance in her tone and body language rather than words that were understood. 'We'd better give you a walk.' Evidently the word walk was well within her vocabulary, because the spaniel attempted a small dance step.

Celia decanted some airgun pellets into the pocket of the waxed-cotton coat and picked up the air rifle. The spaniel began to range to and fro in front of her. 'Oho!' Celia said, and 'Heel.' The spaniel came steadily to heel.

At the far side of the loch she cast the spaniel out. Seconds later a rabbit bolted across her front. She tried, but it was an impossible shot. The spaniel sat tight at the sound. The light was beginning to fade. A moment's consideration told Celia that the wood pigeon would soon be flighting to roost. White splashes under the trees suggested that they were used for the purpose. Pigeon breasts in the freezer compartment of the fridge would be a useful standby. They stood in the concealment of a holly tree and soon the swift shapes began to sweep in against the sky. She waited for them to settle, remembered to aim slightly high and after two misses she scored three times in succession. Told to fetch, the spaniel collected them without hesitation and without showing any sign of trouble with the loose-feathered birds. It was time to stop before the birds came to know better and took to roosting elsewhere.

There was one more task. On her previous foray she had spotted a field of what looked like carrots. It was now dark enough to move around without much risk of being noticed. They followed a field boundary, slipped through a gateway and pulled enough young carrots to make a satisfactory weight in the carrier bag.

They headed for home. It had been a most satisfactory and profitable outing. While she prepared a trout for her own meal, Celia chatted away. The spaniel listened with every sign of interest.

'The way I read you,' Celia said, 'is this. You were professionally trained. You answer to all the conventional commands and don't make any mistakes. Then you were sold to a shooting man. Perhaps you were stolen from him, but I don't think so. He should never have been allowed to own a dog. My dad always said that people should have to pass a test like the driving test before they were allowed to have a dog and now I see what he meant.'

There was a pause while she put the carrots on.

'There's no doubt you've been roughly treated. It's possible that you were lost or wandered off and came into the hands of some rough bugger. You may be microchipped and you could be returned to a loving owner, but I don't think we could risk it. We might be giving you back to the man who thought a good thrashing was a cure for not understanding and that a dog makes a good whipping boy. No, we can't risk that, not at least until we know more.'

When the trout was steaming between two tin plates, she said, 'If you're going to stick around for a while, we need a name for you. Alice? Dorothy? The trouble is that you may not have a girl's name at all.' While she ate and again while she finished the chores she tried names and words that might be used as names but without the spaniel showing any sign of recognition.

They took a short walk together for reasons of hygiene and Celia prepared for bed – once again in near-darkness because she had still not managed to improvise any curtains and lighted windows might very well have attracted attention. When it came to preparing a bed for the spaniel, she was about to raid the cupboards for older clothes when the problem solved itself. The spaniel had already established herself on the bed beside Celia's sleeping bag.

'Oh well! I don't suppose any spaniel was ever cleaner than you are at this moment. At least you haven't been scratching.' On the very edge of sleep, Celia added, 'I meant to live off the land, but you need a more balanced diet. I may have to ditch my principles and make use of some of the tricks my brother Joe taught me. Joe also taught me to be patient but he ended up doing six months because his own patience ran out. I'll have to watch that.'

The spaniel snuffled agreement into her neck.

'You know,' Celia said through a yawn, 'it's good to have company. I wasn't looking forward to weeks or months with only myself to talk to, but I think we'll get along all right. You seem to like the sound of my voice as much as I do and yet you never contradict me, never even inter—'

She broke off in mid-word. She was sound asleep, her nose in the spaniel's soft fur.

Four

Celia was accustomed to waking alone. Tasker O'Neill had usually preferred that she return to her own room. The given reason was that she snored. Celia knew this to be false but she went along with the fiction. One of the duties of a mistress, she felt, was never to contradict. The true fact was that Tasker's dentures hurt and so he took them out to sleep. He was sensitive about being seen in his toothless guise. It was therefore a new experience to Celia to be woken by gentle breathing down her makeshift nightie and the scratch of whiskers on her neck.

The spaniel seemed contented with no more breakfast than a bowl of water flavoured with a little milky tea. While settling for almost as frugal a meal herself Celia continued to try for a reaction to any name, but without provoking any response until aided by coincidence. It was only when, mildly burning her fingers on the teapot, she loudly exclaimed 'Drat!' that she suddenly found the little bitch sitting beside her, quivering expectantly. Then began the long process of trying sounds in the hope of a more certain match. But there are many words rhyming with Drat, few of them names and none of those complimentary. It was just as likely that the bitch had recognized the beginning rather than the end of the ejaculation and here it seemed more hopeful, but the nearest to a positive connection was to 'Dram', an appropriate and cheerful word and one that Celia remembered seeing used for a dog in a novel. So Dram the spaniel remained.

Dram needed exercise and certainly needed to empty herself after the excesses of the previous evening. Celia took her for a walk around the loch. This was interrupted by the discovery of a rabbit in one of the snares. Celia retrieved it and broke its neck with a thrust under its chin, but the episode served to remind her that one person at least was in the habit of visiting her little kingdom, and visiting it at least daily if the law was being observed. It would never do for Dram to be seen and recognized. She reset the snare and they walked on, but she was too thoughtful to pay much heed to the frisking of the spaniel or the progress of the buds. When she had gutted the rabbit and hung it to cool, she settled down with Dram. She clipped the spaniel's ears and trimmed the 'feathering' of her chest and tail. There was still half an inch left in the bottle of hair dye. Using a brush from her makeup kit, she extended several of Dram's black patches especially around the eyes and added a dozen or so spots on her nose. When she had finished she looked until the spaniel began to fidget, but one spaniel can be very like another and the differences were quite enough to divert suspicion.

'Will you be all right if I leave you for an hour or two?' she asked. The question was unnecessary. Dram had already stretched out on the hearthrug, ready to leap into action at the word 'walk' or the sound of a gun; but after a questioning look at her new mistress which she seemed to find satisfactory she had relaxed, just as ready to doze, after the manner of dogs, until it was time to eat or walk again. Celia took up her haversack, locked up and mounted the scooter.

* * *

She topped up the scooter's tank and parked again in the Square at Newton Lauder. Now that she had committed herself to a course of action she would go all the way ... or if not all, most of it. She would have been content to live off the land but a young dog, especially one already suffering from undernourishment, needed a more complete diet. She bought all-in-one dried meal, several supplements, a double dish, a collar and lead, a brush and comb, a dog-nest and a bottle of medicated shampoo. She added one or two toys for chewing. Then and only then, in expectation of soon being back in funds, she shopped for herself.

Her finances were now back at a low ebb. She could only hope that her brothers had taught her well enough. With the load distributed between her haversack and the scooter, the machine's handling had deteriorated until she thought it had become more of an art than a science. She rode with great concentration. If she should fall off, that might make too early an introduction to the locals.

She set off to explore the small town while being careful not to follow the same route more often than could be expected of a stranger searching for an unfamiliar address.

She was looking for a street of a particular category, of valuable properties but not too new. When she had found what she was looking for, she directed her search towards somewhere nearby that the scooter could be left unnoticed and later re-started without wakening sleepers.

Once she was satisfied that all her criteria could be met, she set off for home.

Dram came to the door to greet her but without any hint of anxiety or reproach. It seemed that the spaniel already had absolute confidence in her new keeper. She was clearly desperate to jump up, but it seemed that that temptation had been beaten out of her. She was also getting over a habit of spurting through doors as though she had sometimes been helped through with a kick...

Celia lunched on a sandwich and a yoghurt and lay down to doze away the afternoon. During her time with Tasker O'Neill she had been a night bird; indeed, for much of her life she had been attuned to bedding with the dawn and rising after midday. Her new lifestyle seemed to be heading her back in that direction. Despite the excitement that was beginning to mount, she slept until the shadows were lengthening.

Among her purchases were a roll of black plastic refuse bags and a box of drawing pins. Several of the bags, cut open, were pinned over the windows for blackout and suddenly they had the luxury of being able to use the electric lights without announcing to the world that the cottage was occupied. She prepared a meal for Dram in strict accordance with the instructions on the bag, and another for herself aimed at leaving no smell on the breath.

Dram would need another walk before being shut in again. She turned down the lights and they went out into darkness relieved by faint starlight. As soon as her night vision had returned, she continued her journey down to the loch to feed her refuse to the trout. On the other side of the loch, sometimes reflected in the water, a torch was bobbing among the trees. From her earlier experiences she could recognize the pattern. Soon the torch headed towards the road and vanished. She thought that she could hear an engine.

Dram had taken immediately to her dog-nest and the toys. Celia had only to say, 'Bed,' and the spaniel settled down happily. It was nearly midnight, but Celia recalled that impatience had been her brother's downfall. She had some difficulty riding the scooter along the rough track by the illumination of the rather feeble headlamp. She stopped and gave the lens of the lamp a polish with her sleeve. If she had an accident and fetched up in hospital she might find it difficult to explain some of the tools in her pockets.

As she had hoped, very few lights were showing in the town. She saw no pedestrians at all. In Edinburgh, there would have been taxis and people walking home from clubs and late parties. And the best of luck to them, she thought. The sort of town where people kept regular hours was her sort of place and a haven for would-be burglars.

The small clump of trees that she had earmarked for the bestowal of the scooter had the advantage of being in the middle of a long gradient. Thus, she was able to freewheel silently into position between a big rhododendron and another bush that she judged by the scent to be a philadelphus. She approached her target area on foot. The chosen street was lined with detached houses old enough to be spacious and well built; undoubtedly expensive but not modern enough to be secure. Gardens were large.

The high capital values suggested owners with money. Celia had read the story of Flannelfoot, a successful burglar who had practised his craft for years without being caught, and she had learned some of his lessons. She was interested in cash only, not in offering small valuables for sale around the local pubs. She was still prepared to follow her mother's teachings at least so far as to spare her victims unnecessary loss. Moreover, the best crime is the one that nobody knows has happened. A modest percentage out of every wallet and purse would be put down to absentmindedness or forgetfulness. The loser might not suffer more than a sense of 'I must have passed a twenty in mistake for a ten'. The pitcher might even be able to return to the well although she doubted that the margin of time between the last bedders and the first risers would be time enough for her to work even a quarter of the street. A quite unnecessary moon had broken through. It might save her time but it would increase the very slight risk of being seen by some insomniac.

She bypassed the first house. Loose gravel and a prickly hedge combined to make a silent approach very difficult. The next house was one of the few with a conspicuous alarm system. At the third, a brief flash of her tiny torch through a small window showed a toilet. Her putty knife slipped back the catch of the sash-and-case window. She pulled a pair of Mr O'Neill's black socks over her trainers, donned a pair of latex gloves and a moment later was over the sill. She closed the window, in case some passing policeman might notice it or a breath of air waken the householders, but she left it unlatched.

After making sure that she knew her quickest exit, she went through the house with no more noise than a shadow. The stairs presented a danger but by keeping very close to the side she managed without making more creaks than might be expected from an elderly house in a changing temperature and humidity. Only one bedroom was occupied. The man's clothes were on the chair. His wallet held a few notes. She abstracted a twenty and, once back downstairs, another from the handbag on the kitchen table. She left by the way that she had entered and, using her putty-knife and a piece of nylon fishing line, left the window latched – perhaps not quite as securely as when she had arrived but at least enough so that the house-owner was unlikely to notice. It had been modestly worthwhile but she would have to do better or come again.

The next house had been fitted with replacement plastic windows and double glazing. All the windows were closed and latched. Entry would be possible but not without leaving obvious traces. She moved on to the house next door.

Her entry was almost a copy of the first but the interior conditions were very different. The house was crowded. She seemed to have happened on a family gathering. (Surely they could not live like this all the time?) Every bed seemed fully occupied, including the sofa bed in the sitting room. She stood in the hall, sensing the life around her. The air was exhausted and smelled of drink. Reason first suggested a cautious retreat, but then she decided that people meant wallets and purses to explore and drink meant deep sleep. Upstairs a toilet flushed and boards creaked as somebody returned to bed. That decided her. Any noise that she made would be put down to a visitor heading for a bathroom.

She had to move carefully. Bottles and glasses had been left on tables, chairs and on the floor. But she managed to work her way from room to room, sampling wallets and handbags until she knew that a useful sum must be collecting in her pocket. As she made to leave, she arrived at the head of the stairs. Another toilet flushed. The occupant must have been sitting in silence for a remarkable time. A door opened, spilling light. Celia froze and tried, by sheer willpower, to pull a mantle of invisibility around her. A male figure, tousled, eyes barely open, emerged, clad only in underpants. His heavy eyes settled on Celia. She held her breath. 'I wouldn't go in there just yet,' he said. 'Give it ten minutes.' He gave her a friendly nod and shambled into one of the bedrooms. His breath smelled of booze in several varieties.

As she slipped out of the house and latched the window behind her, she decided he would be unlikely to remember the encounter.

She moved on, but the next house proved impregnable. It retained the old wooden sash-and-case windows but security locks had been added and there would be no way for her to get in without leaving proof that the house had been entered.

The house beyond was an easier proposition. The kitchen window was slightly open and slid up without a sound. The room was warm – evidently the central heating was still at work. The worktop was clear. She sat on it with her feet dangling. Her senses and her reason were suddenly flooded and she realized why the window had been left ajar. There was a padding across the floor, something whiskery was pushed against her hand – she nearly screamed – and she identified the smell in the room as being dog-fart. She knew the smell well enough. A large dog prone to flatulence can taint a room sufficiently to make the eyes water. The only mystery was why any owner should keep the dog in the one room where food was prepared. The reason why the dog had not barked was quite clear as it nosed the pocket in which she kept some dried meal loose, for dishing out piecemeal to Dram as small rewards for obedience on their walks. She held out a small handful with a silent prayer that this dog was not one to snatch or grab. The contribution was lifted gently off her palm.

Cautious use of her small torch revealed that the dog was of no particular breed that she could distinguish but very shaggy and appearing to be about the size of a pony. From the grey jowls and the stiffness of its movements she judged that it was of a considerable age. On a high shelf she saw a large bag of similar dog-meal to what she had in her pocket. She refilled her pocket and gave out another handful.

Night was far advanced. Dawn, and the earliest risers, could not be very far off. This, she decided, would be her last port of call. She eased the kitchen door slightly open and stooped to peer through the gap. Immediately, the dog, who might not have been so very old after all, tried to mount her from behind. Either the dog had smelled Dram on her or she had found a friend. The contact pushed her forward through the doorway but she managed to shut the door between herself and the dog without making more noise than a small click.

At that moment, her well-planned and cautiously executed foray went all to hell.

It must have been the tiny sound of the door latch. Or else a breath of air had roused a sleeper. A table lamp was switched on and somebody yawned prodigiously. The kitchen door, it was now revealed, came off a small hallway opening directly into a large sitting room that seemed to have been made, for purposes of entertainment, by throwing together the original sitting room with a hall and other spaces. A man was beginning to sit up on a huge settee. His face was in the full light. It was round and pink with rose-bud lips, the sort of face that she most disliked on a man; nor was she too enamoured of the fact that he was naked and had been sleeping entwined with a young woman wearing nothing but a bra, stockings and a suspender belt.

He was facing towards her, but he was in the light and Celia was in shade. He lowered his head to pay attention to his companion. If Celia had tried to retreat into the kitchen, the dog would have bounced out. She could only step, very slowly and gently, across the small hallway and settle back against the wall between a coat stand and a hall table. Here, the angle of the wall between the room and the hallway cut her off from his view. A murmuring of endearments gave her some cover as she breathed deeply.

Across that part of the room within her view was the foot of a staircase and what was evidently the front door. And on the wall a small red light blinked in rhythm with the movement of the couple on the settee. It was a shock to match any that she had had that night. The house was fitted with sensors and alarms but the external unit must have been well hidden because she had seen no sign of it. That the system was not yet switched on because of the householder's sex life was possibly fortunate but possibly not. It might yet prove disastrous.

She peeped between the wall and the coat stand. The couple had changed position. The man was now reclining on the settee with the girl kneeling astride and facing him. She was jogging away as though on a trotting horse, but the man's eyes were open and he was facing into the hallway.

She was trapped. She had nothing to do but to look around. On one side of her was the table, which carried nothing but a vase of oriental appearance. On the other side, and more or less hiding her from the man's eyes, was the coat rack. A sheepskin coat, much too warm for the weather, hung on one side. The only other occupied hook held a dark coat. The couple on the couch seemed to be nearing a climax. The trot had become a canter. To take her mind off it, she explored the pockets of the dark coat. There was a fat wallet in the inner pocket.

A narrow beam of light from the table lamp made its way through the gap between the coat rack and the wall. By this poor illumination she checked through the wallet.

A business card showed through a transparent window, reading J. D. Farrow, Dealer in Fine Antiques. The remainder of the bulk was made up of a wad of banknotes, mostly of large denominations. It seemed logical to Celia that a dealer in fine antiques might need to carry a substantial cash float with him in readiness for sudden opportunities and would be unlikely to know exactly how much was in the wallet at any one time. She removed by touch what she thought might be a dozen or so notes and returned the wallet to the pocket. Its bulk did not seem to be much reduced. She was tempted to remove the whole wallet and leave it to Mr J. D. Farrow to assume that he had dropped it or that his pocket had been picked, but her mother's teaching won the day.

The couple on the couch had arrived at the culmination of their efforts. The canter became a gallop. Gasps died to heavy breathing which in turn became sighs of satisfaction. 'God, is that the time?' said the girl. 'It's time I wasn't here.' She disengaged with a soft plop.

'When can you come again?' asked Mr Farrow.

'It may be three weeks before he's away overnight again. I'll phone you.'

The girl had dressed quickly, recovering her clothes from scattered areas of floor. He switched off the table lamp and went to the door with her but turned aside to open a small cupboard. 'What's that?' the girl asked.

'Intruder alarms. When I've set them, I have ten seconds to get upstairs before they detect me as a moving being and go off. Not that I need them really. Brutus – my dog – would see off any intruders.'

Celia smiled quietly to herself. The man was kidding himself or trying to kid the rest of the world. Brutus would welcome anyone who arrived bearing gifts.

The man closed the door behind his guest, set the alarms and hurried upstairs. Celia was tempted to bolt into the kitchen as soon as he was out of sight, but she decided to wait. The detector with its winking red light had been sited, logically enough, with a direct view into the small hall where she stood trapped. An immediate alarm could be disastrous. She had no wish to find herself wrestling with a naked antiques dealer, although she doubted that he would be at his energetic peak. As her night vision increased she saw that the first light of dawn was outlining the windows but still she delayed. Between nerves and the cool of the night she was becoming in need of a pee. It was Tasker O'Neill's sitting room over again.

As soon as she could be reasonably sure, from the sounds percolating down from upstairs, that her unwitting host was in bed, she bolted into the kitchen leaving the door open. She left by way of the window, pulling the upper sash down behind her. Let Brutus, along with an inadequately latched kitchen door, take the blame for the yodelling scream that was making the night hideous. The noise and the strobe light were coming from close under the eaves. Celia was already flitting from garden to garden on her way back to where she had left the scooter. Nobody seemed to be hurrying to look for an intruder. J. D. Farrow might in desperate need of rescue but nobody cared. So much for electronic alarms. Or perhaps he had made himself unloved.

All the same, she would have to be more careful next time. She took a dim view of whoever had designed the alarm system. A more conspicuous positioning of the alarm box would have been a deterrent to such as herself and so would have saved Mr Farrow his interrupted sleep.

She waited until she was hidden beside the

scooter before she relieved herself. White knickers would have shone like a beacon under the moonlight. A milk float jingled by.

Five

The streets seemed deserted. She passed a postman's van. Its driver never looked up. Outside the town, still in the half-light, an owl flitted silently overhead and she slowed to allow a badger to cross on his ambling way home. By the time she reached the mouth of the track the light of dawn had spread.

Her return to the cottage was almost an anticlimax. She opened the door to wheel the scooter inside. Dram came out, yawning, to greet her – not with the relief of a dog that had agonized over being abandoned but the affectionate welcome of the dog that is secure with its keeper. Dram did sniff and give her a reproachful stare, having detected the scent of Brutus, but a walk the short way around the loch was enough for forgiveness and to re-establish loving relations.

Celia, to Dram's disgust, ate a light breakfast and took to her bed. She was in danger of slipping back towards her old habit, formed while being dragooned into helping with her family's more nefarious activities, of sleeping during the evening and morning and waking overnight and through the afternoon. Dram, after the manner of dogs, soon accepted that whatever the reason this was so. She waited until Celia was asleep and then joined her on the bed.

The excitements of the night might have been expected to make Celia restless, but in fact, having solved a major problem – that of finances – she slept like the dead. She woke refreshed. Dram returned to her own bed at the first sign of Celia stirring.

Over a light lunch Celia looked at her overnight haul. At a glance, this seemed to be more than she had expected. Mr Farrow's contribution, which had been judged on thickness without being counted, seemed, on the basis of a quick flick through the corners, to be larger than she had intended; but she comforted herself with the thought, held to be one of life's basic truths in her family, that antiques dealers were all crooks. The total sum obtained, which looked without counting to be somewhere between two and three hundred pounds, would have maintained them in their rent-free lifestyle for some months. Supplemented by trout from the loch, rabbits, vegetables pulled from the fields and, in season, perhaps the occasional pheasant, they could probably survive for a year. The heather round about showed patterns of methodical burning so there would almost certainly be grouse, which Celia knew well how to trap. She would only need a few empty jam jars.

It soon seemed that stress was consigned to history. Without people there was no conflict, no abrasion of the soul. They entered a period of leisure such as Celia hardly remembered. Even a conscientious attention to housekeeping did not make much of a hole in the day. Dram's grooming could be accomplished slowly and thoroughly as a loving ritual. The weather remained fine, so the pair were able to enjoy some long walks, leaving and returning to their own secluded territory by a choice of several inconspicuous ways along tree-strips or dead ground. At other times they sat in the sunshine. Celia's only regret was that she had not brought any reading matter, but the radio at least in part made up for that. She began to take a serious interest in music.

On the fourth day after the raid on Newton Lauder, there was a change in the weather. The day dawned cooler. The sun rose but failed to show. Dark clouds, darker around the horizon, were welling up and prophesying storm and tempest. The wind was rising. Celia wrapped up well, mostly in her late host's clothes, and they took their morning walk early.

By mid-morning the day was like a winter's dusk. Dram decided that night was returning ahead of time and took to her basket, but she kept an eye on Celia for reassurance. At times, the radio was almost drowned by crackling. For lack of any worthier occupation, Celia set to washing and polishing the scooter, which was now seeing little service but stood in the corner between the sitting and kitchen parts of the main room. The electric lights were on but, because it was in theory daytime, the blackouts were not up and the flickers of distant lightning were clearly visible. Celia tried not to count the seconds between the flash and the rumble but she was in no doubt that the storm was coming closer. Dram, who would not have turned a hair at the sound of a shot, quitted her bed and tried to climb on to

Celia's knees.

When it arrived it was ahead of expectation. There was a brilliant flash, a clap of thunder that shook her skull and then the rain was coming down, as pitiless as a rockfall. Glancing outside, she saw the rain rebounding off anything solid and lying in erupting pools over the grass.

Celia took a moment to assure herself that the roof was withstanding the onslaught. She got off her knees to go and close the door in case rain should blow or bounce inside. She paused to re-tune the radio and found that she could get a reasonable signal. By happy chance it was playing Strauss's 'Thunder and Lightning Polka'. Celia laughed and at the end of each line she joined in, crying 'Whizz-bang!' in time with the music. That may have prevented her from hearing the knocking. As she reached the door, she was confronted by a large man with a shotgun.

Celia's heart, or some other organ of similar size, seemed to leap into her gullet and lodge there, fluttering. Her first thought was that the police had arrived. But for which of her various sins, real or apparent, was she in such demand? The theft of the earrings? The stabbing of Mr Jenkins? The taking and driving away of the scooter? Burglary? But common sense asserted itself. The police would hardly have arrived with shotguns to arrest one lonely girl, even one who was clearly guilty of all those crimes.

When her first panic had subsided she saw that he did not mean any mischief. She was acquainted with shotguns. This one was open, the chambers were visibly empty and the man was trying very hard to keep it dry under his armpit. In any case, it was far too antiquated a model for the police to have considered using.

'May I come in? I'm quite harmless.'

To send him back into the pelting rain would only make her an object of curiosity. 'Come in and dry off. Though you couldn't have got much wetter.'

'I could have got even colder.'

He came in, stepping out of his wellingtons at the door. He was wearing a light T-shirt and his jeans had been washed until they were almost threadbare. She brought him a towel, one of the cheap, rough towels that she had found in the cottage. He dried his hair, took off a cartridge belt and then, with a word of apology, dragged off his T-shirt. He was a very large young man and well muscled. Celia got up and went to the cupboards, returning with a long shirt and another towel. 'If you can get into this shirt and tie the towel round your waist, you'll pass,' she said. The sound of the rain was abating but she still had to raise her voice.

'I'd only get just as wet again going home.'

'This rain will pass,' she assured him. 'It always does, in the end.'

'I suppose so.' He was a very good-looking man of around thirty. The curliness of his black hair extended, she had noticed, to his chest. His muscles moved under his skin in a manner that was so natural that it looked almost contrived. Even his jaw muscles seemed prominent. His brown eyes were rather deep-set on either side of a Roman nose. His mouth and chin – a bluish chin, she had to admit – were firm. After a week of solitude, she studied him more intently than she might otherwise have done. His features added up to a face of intelligence and humour. During her periods of enforced idleness her mind had returned to toy, in the abstract, with her earlier idea of writing soft porn. If that should ever come to pass, it occurred to her that he would be a perfect photographic model for the sadistic male protagonist. Yet, with all these advantages and in the presence of an undeniably attractive young woman, he seemed depressed.

He hung his cartridge belt over a chair and retired to the tiny bathroom to make the suggested changes. She put a match to the sticks that had been awaiting their turn in the fireplace during the fine weather. His wet clothes were wrung out and hung on the fireguard and they sat down on either side. He had brought a wad of toilet paper from the bathroom and he set about a meticulous drying of his gun. Another girl might have felt pique, but Celia knew the cost of guns and their repairs and also knew how a man came to associate his gun with all the attributes of masculinity. A proper care for his weaponry, she felt, was quite a proper priority in a man.

'You must have thought I was mad,' she said, 'shouting like that.'

'I thought that it was very appropriate.'

It had become a reasonable time for an early lunch. She got up and boiled the kettle, making a large pot of tea and mugs of soup from packets. She blessed the forethought that had led her to buy sliced ham from the supermarket.

The arrival of soup, sandwiches and tea

seemed to be taken as a signal that conversation was necessary. 'I thought it might rain,' he said, 'but I didn't expect it to bucket down. Dressed lightly, I usually reckon to wet easily and dry easily.' His voice, she noticed, had the accent that she thought of as educated-neutral – the accent to which she aspired with a degree of success that sometimes failed to fool those who spoke that way as of right.

'You'll probably pay for it later,' she said. 'Rheumatism.'

He dismissed rheumatism with a careless movement of his hand. Dram, thwarted of a place on Celia's lap, arrived to pay her respects. He fondled her ears and she groaned with pleasure. 'I could have sworn ... ' he said, regarding the spaniel. 'But no. I'm the keeper,' he added.

'I thought you must be. But you don't sound like a keeper.'

'Probably not. It's a long story.'

'Tell it anyway. This rain isn't going off just yet.'

'I suppose.' He sat back, a half-eaten sandwich in his fingers. 'One life story coming up. I was brought up on a farm not far from here. My dad was determined that I should have an education. He sent me to good schools. I went on to university and got a good degree in biological science.' His hand had drooped over the arm of the chair. He rescued his sandwich before Dram could take the benefit of it, changed hands and absently fondled the spaniel's ear. 'I was doing postgraduate research into gapeworm in pheasants. Suddenly I realized that I didn't want to spend the rest of my life in laboratories and lecture theatres. I had been brought up in fresh air and that's where I wanted to be. Can you understand that?' He looked at her with his brown eyes as pleading as those of Dram.

'I can understand it very easily,' Celia said.

'I decided that I wanted the life of a keeper. I would be taking a large drop in pay and status. The money didn't matter – I had something saved and I would come into something from my father in the fullness of time. There are courses I should have taken, I realize that now. But I answered an advertisement for an assistant keeper here and got the job.' He fell silent.

'You don't sound as if you're as happy as you expected.'

'It's a good life. But the keeper, Jim McKee, knew his stuff, yet he couldn't teach it. That's often the way – the man who knows it can't teach it. And vice versa, I'm sorry to say. He'd give me the simple tasks, telling me to go and do this or fetch that while he got on with the skilled jobs. And the money was rubbish. I suppose I was stupid, but I had married and I suppose I couldn't blame my wife for resenting being penniless.'

'Usually a keeper's income is largely made up of tips from guests and visitors.'

'So I was told. But the tips were given to Jim; and Jim hung onto them. I think the farm manager always paid me in cash so as not to get involved with stamping cards and PAYE. He could have landed us both in trouble. I'm paid by cheque now, though it's not a lot more. Just to make ends meet, my wife had to cycle into Newton Lauder and do cleaning jobs.'

'That's awful,' Celia said. 'She must have hated that.'

'Not as much as you might think. You see, she'd been one of the maids in a hall of residence at the university, so she was quite used to that sort of work. She'd never known any other. But she was also devastatingly attractive, so I married her. What she thought she was marrying was status and prospects and I'd thrown them up.

'Then, last January, Jim McKee had a

heart attack and retired suddenly and I was told that the job was mine.'

'She'll be happier now,' Celia commented.

'She ... isn't here now.'

The rain was still pattering on the roof and gusts of wind whirled it against the windows. Although they had only just met, in the warm cocoon surrounding the fireplace a sort of intimacy was developing and she could sense that this was a subject that he did not want pursued. 'Perhaps you'll be happier now,' she substituted.

'In a way, yes. I like the place. I've inherited the keeper's cottage, which is less of a slum than the assistant keeper's hovel. I've got it more or less cleaned out and arranged pretty much the way I want it. I like the work. But – dammit! – I'm not ready for it. I don't have the practical experience. I know the theory. I've got the books. But have you noticed that the books always start from the assumption that you have an understanding of the subject and know all the jargon?'

She smiled. 'I think everybody must have noticed that. It's universal experience.'

'Well, I've been struggling to get the release pens ready and now the laird has ordered an extra four hundred poults and he wants me to put up a release pen somewhere around here and I don't know where to begin.'

She heard her own voice saying, 'Perhaps I can help. My father was a keeper.' Not a word was said about her father's fall from grace.

He looked at her for a moment as though she had suddenly materialized, clad in a minimum of silk and lace and carrying a tray of rich food and drink. 'Oh? Would you do that?' He seemed to be holding his breath in case she withdrew the suggestion.

'I don't see why not. Tell me, who is the laird?'

He seemed startled that she had to ask the question but he was too much of a gentleman to press the point. 'Simon Watson, MP. He has quite a sizeable estate between here and Newton Lauder.'

'I've met him,' Celia said. 'Not a bad old stick. You must go and see him or his agent at once. It would be absolutely normal for the farms to provide a little help and be paid for it.'

'No problem there. The biggest farmer's a member of the syndicate.'

'So much the better.'

'Your fire's going out,' he said.

'I don't have any more logs. But your

clothes are dry enough. When the rain's off we'll go and look for a site, make a list of materials and then you go off to demand help and support and the purchase of posts and wire mesh. The birds will want somewhere not too damp, with a sunny area and some cover where they can hide from predators and a shelter in case this weather comes back. They need perches so that they can learn to roost off the ground. There's a good place just across the loch. And if you can't borrow from the other pens, you'll need some extra feeders and drinkers. I hope you've got feed on order.'

He had been listening raptly as she spoke – so raptly that he had been unaware that the towel around his waist had begun to gape. She had been on the point of warning him to cover up, but she could hardly have helped noticing that he was singularly well hung. She had no objection to the spectacle. She had seen such things in the past and, on occasions, had found them to be a source of comfort and pleasure.

'The sun's coming out,' he said wonderingly. As relief dawned something else was stirring, but even if he had made a move this was not the time for dalliance. That time might some day come. She was detecting an inner person who she could like, inside a shell that was definitely attractive. If the attraction was mutual, time alone would tell.

'Come on,' she said quickly. 'Let's go and take a look at the place.'

The sun came fully out. Celia put on extra socks and the late Mr O'Neill's green wellingtons. Puddles began to steam. Dram danced with excitement, creating her own rainbows.

Six

Celia was quite accustomed to being awoken by the birdsong which is always prevalent on keepered territory. She slept through it next morning and was woken by Dram. Dram was in a state of excitement, having acquired Celia's nervousness about visitors. She had been roused by the arrival from the direction of the road of a Toyota pickup laden with fence posts, rolls of wire mesh, tools and sundry other materials.

Remembering previous experiences, Celia dragged on a pair of jeans with an urgency that nearly lifted her feet off the ground and shot outside, barefoot and with her hair as unkempt as a heron's nest. The driver, who, just as she had suspected, had been about to dump the load at the gable of the cottage and leave it for anyone who cared to carry it all round the loch the hard way, was not pleased to be chased back into his driving seat, joined aboard by the same termagant, directed round the loch and over the stream by way of a bridge contrived from old railway sleepers and ordered to unload at three different points. She then insisted on a lift back to the cottage before allowing him to go about his other duties.

She was not going to be caught again. She washed quickly, dressed as smartly as the occasion would allow and was in the middle of breakfast when two farmhands arrived on a quad bike accompanied by a forester on a motorcycle. These, she gathered, had been lent to them for one day only. Taking up a mug of tea in one hand and a slice of toast and marmalade in the other, she trotted ahead of them to the site for the release pen. She marked out the positions for the posts and left the farmhands to drive them in with podger and maul. The forester, who seemed to have some idea of what it was all about, she left to fabricate two mesh-covered gates and some grids for pop-holes carefully sized for a pheasant to pass and a fox to be thwarted.

Before returning to the cottage to finish her breakfast, she left the forester to get on with his gates and went to see how the farm-hands were getting on. They seemed glad of the excuse to break off for a chat, but they had set up a remarkable number of the posts very firmly so she could hardly grudge them a respite. What she could grudge them were certain topics of conversation.

The younger farmhand was round-faced, rubicund and cheerful. He looked down at Dram. 'Han't I seen that dug afore?' he asked.

Celia cringed secretly. A dog's marking may be altered but to the dog-lover such things as habit and posture remain unchanged. 'One spaniel looks much like another,' she said.

'I suppose.'

The elder of the two was a small man with a malevolent expression and a curious disposition. 'You and Kenny Whetstone will be a couple, no doubt?' he asked with a smile that could almost have been a leer.

'You needn't try your hand, then, Gerry,'

the younger man said.

'Twenty years back ... ' said the older man. He seemed to feel that the sentence was not in need of completion.

'I only met him a couple of days ago,' Celia said. Even that was doubling the true period of their acquaintance.

'Long enough,' said the older man.

'For some,' said the younger. It seemed that they had worked together for long enough to have established a truncated form of conversation.

However true either remark might be, it was not a topic that Celia cared to pursue with her helpers. She gave them careful instructions as to how the posts should be wired and the mesh hung. As she walked away, she heard the older man speaking to her back. 'Ask him what became of his wife.' The other man hushed him. She pretended not to hear.

The forester was working intelligently and progressing well. She went back to the cottage.

So the keeper was Kenny Whetstone. As names go, it was passable. But where had he got to? To be sure, she had given him enough errands to keep him going for days, but to bugger off without a word, leaving her to direct the operations of a bunch of cack-handed novices, that was a bit much. She would have a serious word with him when he returned. If he returned. Meantime, however, work must go on.

She finished her breakfast and attended to the few chores. The men did not seem to have brought the usual haversacks or lunch boxes. This was not going to be an excuse to knock off and go home for an hour or two. A mid-morning snack would give her a chance to find out. The cupboard under the sink had contained two thermos flasks. She rinsed them with boiling water and then filled them with tea. Another cupboard furnished a hip flask, which could hold milk. She put a packet of biscuits into one pocket and sugar, in a twist of paper, in the other and washed out some mugs.

Back at the release-pen site, work was proceeding but without any sense of urgency. It picked up pace while she was present to supervise and to fetch and carry tools, nails and staples. She dispensed tea. The farm-hands claimed that they had expected to be working close to their respective homes and would need to go back to eat. She said that food would be provided. The older man said that he would have to go and tell his wife that he would be absent for lunch.

She had used the last of her bread, so sandwiches were out. The cupboards, she knew, contained a can of goulash (purloined from Tasker O'Neill's flat) and a larger can of baked beans. She was wondering what else there might be that could be incorporated into some sort of stew or casserole to go around three men, plus Ken Whetstone if he should ever return, plus, as an afterthought, herself, although she could make do on the remains of last night's trout. She was about to set off back to the cottage when a rusty Land Rover pickup approached the cottage and then turned to follow the path that was developing towards the release-pen site.

She met and halted it. Ken Whetstone was at the wheel. She leaned in at the window. 'Where the hell have you been?' she demanded in a low tone. She had learned years earlier never to row in front of the helpers.

'Took longer than I thought,' he said. 'And you aren't on the phone at Loch Cottage. I brought you some bread and things, by the way, and there are logs for you in the back under the mirrors.'

'Mirrors?'

'Yes. I did as you told me,' he said plaintively. 'I phoned the furniture dealer and auctioneer to ask about mirrors. He said they'd been collecting for years and he's planned to put them to the tip but I could have the lot for a fiver. So I went there straight away and collected about a dozen mirrors, most of them wardrobe-door size and two of them huge. They all have corners cracked off but—'

'That doesn't matter,' Celia said.

'But what do you want them for?' He climbed down. For his long legs, it was not much of a climb.

'I'll explain later. I've had my hands full. You left me to get the work started here.'

'I knew you could cope.'

'But these twirrups had to be supervised every moment. They didn't know which way was up.'

He rounded on the two farmhands, who were trying to look invisible. 'They were having you on,' he said. 'Jim McKee always had the use of those two when he was over-stretched.'

The younger man muttered something about a joke.

Celia was delighted to see that, for the first time, he was showing confidence and authority. 'A joke, was it? We'll see how funny your boss thinks it is, when I tell him that you pretended not to know the job, just to make life difficult for a young girl.' He took a good look at the work already done. 'And when I tell him that she turned out to know the job a damned sight better than either of you ... '

'You're not going to clype on us!' said the older man.

Ken was grim. 'Maybe. Maybe not. Not if you get stuck in and do a proper day's work.'

Celia decided to stick her oar in before Ken was forced to reveal his ignorance. 'When you've finished with the wire mesh, you can gather stones and fallen branches to weight the bottom down where it turns outward. We want this fox-proof. Now,' she said to Ken, 'unload a couple of smaller mirrors or one big one and give me the bread and doings. We've got time before lunch. Let's go round the other release pens and see what needs doing.'

'I've been attending to them.'

'That's good, but let's see if we can't make them even better.'

He hesitated, wondering whether male pride called for a show of indignation. But her help was worth so much more than a pretence of superiority. He turned back to the Land Rover. 'Let's do that,' he said.

* * *

They left the carrier bag of food in the cottage and set off again. As they bumped along the track with new growth scraping the Land Rover's underside, he asked, 'What are the mirrors for?'

'You're not allowed to shoot birds of prey any more. Have you seen how their numbers are building up? Sparrow hawks and buzzards, mostly, around here. We could net the tops of the pens, but that's laborious and expensive and the chicks will need to get outside the pens before they're too big for a sparrowhawk to take. But they'll need shelters from really bad weather, and if you top off each roof with a mirror it frightens the predators off. A sparrowhawk coming in for an easy meal sees another bird of prey approaching from an impossible angle and gets the fright of its life. They don't usually come back.'

'Clever,' he said.

She was pleased to approve four release pens. They were satisfactorily impregnable, with the topmost foot of mesh turned outwards and loose to present an impassable obstacle to cats climbing over. There was a large drum at each, ready to be filled with grain for topping up the smaller feeders. The shelters were already there. They selected mirrors of suitable size to leave at each and when the back of the Land Rover was empty except for logs they combined to wrestle a large drum and some sheets of corrugated asbestos aboard.

Returning by a different route, he showed her his stone-built cottage, backed by neat sheds. It was set in a walled garden which was running to seed. Ken said, defensively, that the keeper's job was enough for one man on his own without trying to keep a garden as well. The cottage stood on the most important of the farm roads and was surrounded by fields. The rolling contours lent themselves to woods and spinneys that had been established on the higher ground by far-sighted Victorians, embellishing the look of the countryside and, more importantly, offering the chance to drive very high birds over the Guns. The cottage faced south, looked well built and fitted charmingly into its surroundings. Some buildings manage to look happy, and this was one of them.

She would have liked to see the inside but he was preparing to drive off. She had been reminded of the older farmhand's remark.

'What happened to your wife?' she asked.

The Land Rover hesitated and then went on. 'She just vanished,' he said. 'There was never an explanation. It's not something I like to talk about.'

'I don't suppose you would,' she said. She cast around for another subject. 'Have you been using snares around the loch?'

Unconsciously he let the Land Rover slow a little. 'No,' he said. 'I have not.'

'There are snares there, sometimes. Set for rabbits. Then they disappear again. You're being poached.'

They picked up speed again. 'I don't suppose the estate will miss a few rabbits.'

'I wouldn't suppose so,' she said. 'But if you leave him to get on with it, do you think he'll leave the pheasants alone?'

In the carrier bag he had brought sliced wholemeal bread and various fillings. Celia made what she guessed would be enough sandwiches and thriftily stored the leftover materials in the fridge. She carried the sandwiches and flasks of tea down to the release pen. Ken had made a start to building a low shelter from the corrugated sheets topped by the mirrors.

They became a friendly party over the

sandwiches. Celia and Ken sat on a fallen tree trunk; the others squatted on the ground. When the last crumb and the last gulp of tea had gone down, the men returned almost willingly to work. Another hour saw it finished to her satisfaction. The men, it seemed, were preparing to knock off.

'Hold your horses,' Celia said. 'We've only got you for the one day.'

'And you work one day,' Ken said, 'or we complain to your boss. There are bags of grain in the barn for distributing around the release pens and guess who's going to load and unload the Land Rover.'

'We always knock off about now,' said Gerry, the older farm worker. 'See, we're up in the morn before some folk are stirring.' Ken produced a bulky and old-fashioned mobile phone. 'Oh, very well, very well,' Gerry said angrily.

They worked until the light went. By that time the drums were full. Ken had to drive Celia back to the Loch Cottage, as she now knew it to be, so she invited him in. 'Could you get by on sandwiches again?' she asked him. 'If so, you can stay for supper.'

'Sounds like heaven.'

She was finding him an attractive man. Being able to teach him something about his job did nothing to diminish his appeal. After a day in wellingtons, however, even a saint would have smelly feet, or such was her experience. There were men's slippers in the wardrobe and she brought them to him.

'If you were a real gentleman,' she said, 'you'd make the sandwiches while I have a shower.'

His face broke up into a broad smile, transforming itself from merely handsome to something very special. 'I am a real gentleman,' he said, 'and I'll make the sandwiches.'

They ate in front of the fireplace again, where several of the new logs were making warm patterns of light. Dram, newly fed, dozed in the warmth.

'I had a look. I could see where one or two wire snares have been set,' he said.

'That would add up,' she said. 'He – whoever it is – seems to come one day and set his snares. Then he comes the next day, lifts them and stays away for a few days. He'll probably come tonight.'

He finished his share of the sandwiches and picked up his mug. 'I'll be busy when the birds have been delivered.'

'That you certainly will. How did Jim

McKee manage? Just by borrowing farm-hands?'

'He had me to help, even if he didn't make effective use of me. There were working parties now and again. I think he got the syndicate members to turn out and help. He grumbled that one or two of them were too high and mighty to get their hands dirty, but most of them are down-to-earth locals who understand that a bit of work's good for the shooting and helps to keep the subscriptions down.'

'Why don't you have them helping you just now?'

He looked uncertain. 'I don't even know them. Jim McKee had me controlling the beaters' line while he looked after the Guns.'

'And the tips. I think you'd better speak to Simon Watson, or whoever's the chairman.'

Ken was nodding. 'He'll be here at the weekend.' But his mind was on more immediate matters. 'I think I'll stay up tonight and wait for the poacher. I could be quite comfortable in the Land Rover, even sleep for a while.'

'I'll stay with you,' she said. 'That way we can sleep in turns. Anyway, you shouldn't go against poachers on your own. You need a witness and somebody to use your mobile phone. Only leave your Westley Richards at home. A punch-up is permissible but a gun battle must not happen. I'm handy with a pick handle, bring one for me and I'll bring more sandwiches.'

'You never cease to surprise me. How did you know that my gun was by Westley Richards?'

'I recognized the doll's head extension. That's an old gun. Has it ever been proved for nitro powder?'

'I never thought about it. How do you tell?'

'Show me the gun some time and I'll tell you from the proof marks.' It passed through her mind that Simon Watson, or whoever acted as syndicate secretary, had to have been mad to appoint a keeper who knew all the theory and none of the practice. But still, every man needs a good woman to keep him straight. 'You'd better learn something about proof marks,' she said, 'just in case somebody turns up with a gun that's out of proof.'

'The syndicate's guns are mostly new. I've seen the members assembling.'

'The beaters, then. You'll be expected to host at least one day for beaters and pickers-up at the end of the season.'

'There's only two paid beaters on syndicate days – the two farmhands we had the use of today. The same when it's the laird's own shoot. The rest of the beating is done by the wives, girlfriends, uncles and cousins of the Guns and by the Guns taking turns. When it's a let day, we borrow the beaters from the estate next door. It used to belong to Sir Peter Hay but it passed to his daughter.'

When Celia's father had been a keeper it had been on what she considered to be a proper shoot, with a full team of beaters, double Guns and loaders. She had expected better from a Member of Parliament – and a Westminster MP at that, not just one of the Edinburgh contingent. But still, his lot weren't in government just now so he wouldn't have so many opportunities to line his pockets, which, in her father's opinion, must be the only motivation for entering Parliament.

Seven

Celia, who was wondering when, if ever, she would get another cooked meal, made more sandwiches, tea and soup, all aimed at maintaining warmth and morale during a long wait in the cold night. She wrapped herself up well. Ken had gone back to the keeper's cottage for a wash and to gather up some blankets. As they had arranged, after she had let Dram out and then settled her on her bed, Celia walked up to the largely coniferous woodland that straddled the approach track. Ken was quite positive that the poacher was not anyone from the immediate locality and there was no other approach suited to a visitor in a vehicle, even a four-by-four.

The trees made the black night blacker. Even with the rechargeable lantern, she could feel the darkness clinging around her, its silence suffocating. Creatures of the night are nocturnal because they are predatory or prey, and there would be little point choosing darkness for concealment and then advertising one's presence and position by noise. The only living creatures seemed to be midges, which navigated by scent and homed in on the sweat caused by an uphill walk and in rather more clothes than the night so far required. She jumped but felt relief when a blink of the Land Rover's lights showed that she had reached the gap in the trees where Ken planned to lay his ambush. He put on the interior light until she had climbed into the passenger's seat.

'Are you warm enough?' he asked solicitously.

'Too warm, if anything. Are you hungry?'

'Not yet.'

Each having made polite enquiry into the other's comfort, conversation lapsed. Ken had always believed that the need to 'make conversation' was mildly insulting, suggesting that the other person did not believe him to have the mental resources to be silent without being bored. But while confined in a small space with a member of the opposite sex, that view seemed harsh. The silence may have provided the spur that goaded him into saying, 'You asked what happened to my wife. I may as well tell you.'

She suddenly thought that she might be happier not knowing. 'Not if you don't want to.'

'I want to. I don't want you thinking things. I'll tell the story so far as I know it, which isn't all the way. If you believe me, that's it behind us. If you don't, then we didn't have much of a future anyway.'

The assumption that they might have a future slotted neatly into her own thinking, but she had been turning away from any such thoughts. She was a criminal on the run, she reminded herself, even if the crimes that she had committed were much less than the crimes for which the police would be hunting her. On the other hand, the concept was comforting and not lightly to be put aside, now that he had made mention of it. Amid such conflict it was difficult to think of a coherent answer, so she made none.

Ken seemed to take her silence for agreement. 'I blame myself,' he said into the darkness. 'We married when I was doing my research work. She was young but very attractive and very sexy. If we weren't exactly rolling in money at least we got by. We loved each other, or I thought we did. We certainly behaved that way towards each other. She was, or is, a very intense person, sometimes rather selfish but capable of great generosity when the mood was right. She seemed to enjoy meeting an intellectual class of person – people who were on the way up. Mad as hatters, some of them, outside their own lines of expertise, but she didn't see that. She could be very passionate in ... you know what I mean.'

'In the bed?'

'Well, yes. Eventually, I explained to her that I found the academic life stultifying and that I wanted a more hands-on job. She probably didn't appreciate that this would mean a hand-to-mouth existence tucked away in a cottage at the butt end of a Borders farm. I can't blame her for that. Even I didn't guess what an unfair deal I'd be given. She seemed to go along with it all. But, of course, we were still in what you might call the honeymoon stage. The assistant keeper's cottage must have come as a shock to her. Dark, damp and draughty. She understood nothing about my life and she didn't want to know. She asked me once what was the point of raising all the birds just to shoot them.'

Celia had grown up quite understanding that birds were a crop to be raised and harvested like any other. If people with money were prepared to spend it on participating in the process, that kept all the wheels turning. To shoot was the lasting survival of the hunt which had once been, along with the feast that would follow, the high point of the hunter-gatherer's life. She made a sound of disapproval that Ken accepted as a proper comment.

'To cut a long and miserable story short,' he said, 'she was unhappy but not as unhappy as all that. To make ends meet, she used to cycle into Newton Lauder and worked as a "daily woman" for some of the better-heeled families. I never spied on her but she was never absolutely without her little luxuries like clothes and makeup. I managed to convince myself that some of those things were passed on to her by the lady of one house or another. Now I'm fairly sure that those things were gifts from men, not the result of immoral earnings, but I couldn't be sure.

'She began spending more and more time away from home. And people began to drop hints. I could no longer ignore the fact that she had a lover, possibly more than one. To be honest, I no longer cared. We had stopped sleeping together. Being a figure of fun or pity, a cuckold, didn't bother me in the least. As long as she helped me out with a little cooking and cleaning, I considered myself to be ahead of the game.

'Late last summer, it happened. We'd had some trouble with poachers, rather more serious than what we're dealing with just now. It came to a fight but there was never a prosecution because we hadn't gathered useable evidence. Mr Gracie, the estate manager, on the laird's instructions, sent me on a weekend course about the keeper and the law. Very interesting it was too. Mr Gracie's the person nominally in charge of the shoot as well as all the other estate business, although the laird, Mr Watson, makes most of the decisions.

'When I came back there was no sign of my wife. I can't say that I was surprised and I was really too busy to bother much, with the season just about to open. Jim had me dashing all over the place doing the things he'd forgotten, getting peg numbers and sewelling ready, checking over the beater's van, ordering cartridges and so on. I learned to cook in a hurry, bought a lot of pre-prepared meals from the supermarket and got by. At least I had only my own mouth to feed, but against that she'd gone off with a receipt in her pocket that I needed for Mr

Gracie. I was reimbursed in the end for what I'd spent on Fenn traps, but he grudged it.

'About three weeks later two detectives, a sergeant and a constable, arrived, wanting to question me. In point of fact, they arrived on the morning of the first shoot of the season, an important occasion.'

She knew how busy a keeper would be on such a day. 'The last straw?' she suggested.

'Not far off it. I'd better explain that the season's shoots are divided between let days, which help to offset the costs, syndicate days and two days each season that the laird keeps for himself and his guests. This was one of the laird's days and as you can imagine his guest list was made up of nobs, fellow MPs and so on, one or two nearby landowners who'll return the invitation and one or two syndicate members. Mr Watson wasn't pleased to have the police about the place. He pointed out that my wife had been absent for several weeks and there was nothing significant about that particular day. He sent them away with fleas in their ears. But they came back the next day, of course. I answered all their questions and the sergeant seemed satisfied.

'The detective constable wasn't satisfied, not by a mile. It was soon obvious that he thought I'd killed her. I suppose his superiors don't agree and would prefer to let the matter drop, but they can't order him to back off just in case there turns out to be something in it. There's never been a fatal-accident enquiry so it's still open. He came back asking question after question, usually the ones I'd already answered. He spent a lot of time poking around on his own, looking for places that a body could be buried or hidden. He had me row him round and round the loch for a whole day while he dragged a grapnel through the mud, disturbing the fish, upsetting the habitat and finding absolutely nothing except a couple of tyres. He still comes back, now and again, when he thinks of a new question or a new place to look.'

Celia had given her whole attention to listening, evaluating his tone of voice and looking for contradictions. During the telling, they had somehow come to link hands although she could not recall who had initiated the move. She found the sincerity that flowed through the contact just as convincing as his voice. 'I believe you,' she said.

'I'm glad.' There was a pause. 'Your turn,' he said huskily. He gave the hand that he was still holding a gentle shake.

Celia came down to earth with a jolt. She had come to suppose that he was accepting her as somebody who happened to occupy the cottage. 'Me?' she said.

'Yes, of course. Listen, I don't mind what's in your past but I want to know. I can't live any other way.' He gave her hand a small shake. 'There's something there. You're upset, I can sense it, but you'll feel better once it's out. Perhaps we can sort it out together. And now you want to know how I know you have a problem. Don't worry, it's not telepathy, it's body language. It's the way you jumped when I walked in on you. And you're showing fair hair at your parting. A dark-haired girl may bleach her hair but no blonde would ever dye her hair black without a good reason. You'd better do something about your parting if you're going to mix with people. You're quite tall for a girl but a lot of men are taller. Now, how do you come to be staying in Mr O'Neill's cottage? Are you his ... um ... girlfriend?'

'I'm not anybody's um anything,' she said. 'Not now. And I don't know which Mr O'Neill you mean. But yes, I was the girlfriend of the Mr O'Neill who owns the cottage now, the nephew of the one who used to own it but died. And if that bothers you, say so now.'

She felt him chuckle. 'I wish that I could have met you before you'd ever had any romance in your life at all. But life isn't like that. For most of us, that would mean meeting in our teens. Not many of us have an uncontaminated past. I've been married. For all I know I still am. I'll accept you for what you are now if you'll do the same for me.'

His voice, coming out of the darkness, was so reasonable that she was reassured. 'If it's any help, I'm not pregnant, I don't have any children and I've never had any nasty infections.' She realized that her voice had become very small.

She felt him chuckle. 'I was sure of it. Now tell the tale.'

'It's a long story,' she said. She found that her mouth had gone dry. She was about to repay his trust with a much greater confidence. 'Let's have coffee while I tell it.' When two mugs of coffee were sharing their warmth, she began at the very beginning and told him the story of the man who drove her to defend herself with the bottle. 'I never meant to injure him badly,' she said. 'I just wanted to chase him away. The court accepted my version and I only got probation. But it was on my record.'

She went on to explain her relationship with Tasker O'Neill. 'I'm not proud of myself,' she said. 'But I'd got myself into a depressed state, I couldn't make ends meet and all I could see for myself was a lifetime of drudging away at a word-processor. A little security seemed like a very big deal even if a wedding ring wasn't part of the deal.'

'You don't have to justify yourself to me,' Ken said. 'Most relationships, most marriages, are an exchange of sex, with or without housekeeping, for security, protection and companionship. Friendship plus sex becomes love.'

'You're cynical,' Celia said, 'but I suppose you have a right to be. And I can't say that you're wrong. Anyway, we rubbed along on that sort of understanding until a week or so ago, although friendship may have been a bit sparse. I was more a trophy than a companion.' She explained, carefully and dispassionately, how she had been tricked into modelling the earrings and contributing to their theft.

As she came to the story of how she had been surprised and taped to the chair she felt him stiffen; but when she reached the treatment meted out to her by Tasker O'Neill his indignation became focused. 'The selfish, arrogant, cruel bastard,' he said. 'Would you like me to sort him out for you? He's bound to visit his cottage before he sells it.'

She shook her head, although the gesture was wasted in the darkness. 'One thing I've learned is that revenge pays no dividends. There's no point both of us being in trouble. Anyway, you'd only draw attention to where I'm staying now. Whenever I feel that revenge might be sweet, I still have a key to his flat. I could sneak in and use his computer, connect it to the Internet, fill it up with child porn and give the police an anonymous tip-off.'

She felt him shake with laughter. 'You wouldn't really do that, would you?'

'Probably not,' she admitted after a moment's thought. 'It takes me two days to get angry. For that long, I'm usually feeling guilty and wondering if it's all my fault. Then I start to cool down again. If I didn't do it last week I'll probably never do it at all. Not unless he treats me badly again.'

The night was becoming cold but he did not run the engine in case the noise gave warning to their quarry. She opened the box of sandwiches and poured more coffee, but her teeth were soon chattering. Even the addition of two blankets did little to ward off the chill. 'A good cuddle would be the best medicine,' he said. However, a Land Rover pickup of that vintage is not conducive to cuddling. The central box may be a convenient repository for odds and ends and give access to the transfer box but it gets seriously in the way of certain other activities; and, of course, a standard pickup has no back seat. 'I'll take you on my knee,' he said.

Celia had no objection to such an arrangement but there was a snag. 'I don't want to get out into the cold,' she said. 'I'll freeze.'

'You don't have to. I'm coming over. Lift your bum.'

With some difficulty he managed to scramble over the box and the gear levers and to insert himself beneath her. After adjusting the seat, she was surprised to find that she had adequate headroom. With the available blankets wrapped around the two of them, they began to warm up.

'You might have been better to have ridden it out,' Ken said. 'Flight is usually taken as evidence of guilt.'

'There was still a delay of eight or nine

hours after the stabbing and before I could have contacted the authorities.'

'You had an explanation for that.'

She sighed. Ken, who had been warming his hands inside her coat, was entranced by the soft movement. She said, 'The only evidence I would have had to support that explanation would have been Tasker's, and I don't see him giving it. He isn't the sort to get involved if he can possibly avoid it.'

'The more you tell me about him, the less I like him.'

'I've rather gone off him myself. Perhaps I will use my key after all.'

The silence that followed was broken only by the sound of their breathing. At last Ken said, 'You know that I fancy you like mad?'

She wriggled in what she hoped was a ladylike manner. 'I should bloody well hope so, the way your hands have been wandering around. I wouldn't want to think that you behave like that with every passing female.'

She felt him chuckle again. 'Well, I don't. I don't know what's come over me except that you seemed to be accepting my – what shall I say? – caresses in pretty much the spirit in which they're delivered.'

'Which is?'

'Gratitude. Admiration. Love. Lust. Take

your pick.'

'I think I like them all,' she said, 'but the last one would do for now.' She twisted round on his lap and offered her lips for a kiss. He must have been hoping for it because he had made time for a shave.

Sitting on his lap, she could hardly fail to know what she was doing to him. It was in both their minds that only a few layers of clothing lay between body parts that were becoming charged with anticipation. She moved gently, insinuatingly, to and fro and she heard him groan. What might have happened, even in the confines of the Land Rover, would be anybody's guess, but they were thoroughly interrupted. The sound of an approaching vehicle had been impinging on their consciousness, but each had pretended not to hear rather than break the intimacy of the moment. If the vehicle passed them and went down to the loch it would be trapped.

It did not go past.

The Land Rover's windows were steamed up, but something in the change to the darkness made Celia break off a kiss that was turning into a contest to see who could be first to swallow the other. She offered him an ear to nibble while she wiped the windscreen. The approaching vehicle was very poorly lit. It seemed to be silhouetted against its own light and yet it was not travelling in reverse. Even so there was no doubt that it was turning into the gap in the trees where Ken was parked.

Ken just had time to let off his parking brake. There was a last-moment slither on pine needles and then a metallic crunch. Ken's Land Rover was shunted back but he and Celia were crammed in too tightly to be thrown around.

'Let me out of here,' Ken said grimly. He sounded breathless.

'You sit where you are,' Celia said. 'I know that vehicle. Leave this to me.'

'You're here because tackling poachers is a two-person job.'

'Not this one.'

She turned and slipped out of the cab, re-fastening the waistband of her jeans as she went. She had stopped feeling cold but as she went, walking on shaking knees, she found that freezing draughts were finding apertures in her clothing where none had been earlier. She tried to twitch her clothes back into their proper disposition. At some time, Ken seemed to have managed to un-hook her bra but that was of no importance under her layers of clothing and in the darkness. She could now see, as she suspected, that the other vehicle's only light showing was a lamp fitted below the rear of the car and shining forward – an old poacher's trick whereby just enough light is thrown forward to steer by at slow speeds but almost none escapes to be seen from a distance and number plates are invisible.

The other driver had stalled. She reached in through his open door and removed the key. 'I thought so,' she said. 'Come out of there, you old bugger.'

A burly figure well wrapped in waxed cotton emerged. 'Joan?' it said. 'Is that you?'

'Of course it's bloody well me. I'm with the keeper, so be careful what you say. Give me a hundred quid to fix the damage and we'll say no more. You won't want to refer this to your insurance company, if you have one.'

'Where would I get that sort of money?'

'You always carry that and more on you, in case you get the chance of some dubious deal. Lights,' she called to Ken. They were flooded with light.

He produced a fat wallet and counted out a mixture of denominations. 'I'll be going, then.'

'You wait,' said his daughter. 'I can guess what you're doing here. You've been visiting one of your fancy women out this road and setting a few snares on the way to give yourself an alibi. Well, you can put the word about that this is my patch. Have the police been at you or Mum, asking about me?'

'No. Why would they?'

'Never you mind why. If they do ... ' She considered for a moment. He knew who she was with. A little further information to her father would do little harm. 'If they do, you don't know where I am. Then you phone ... What's your phone number?' she asked Ken.

'Seven six eight two.'

'I can remember that,' said her father.

'See that you do. Now, unless you want me to tell Mum all about your goings-on, you'll remove your snares and go. If you ever come back, come with a collar and tie on and knock on the front door.'

'Which front door?'

'That's for you to find out. You may as well drive down to the loch now. You can use your lights. There's nobody there.'

'What shall I tell your mum?'

'Tell her nothing at all. I'll contact her in my own sweet time, but don't tell her that. You've never seen me. Got it?'

'I've got it.' He paused and looked at her by the Land Rover's lights. 'A right chip off the old block you are,' he said.

She told him where to go and turned away. She heard him reverse his vehicle and drive off towards the loch. Ken had already transferred to the driver's seat. She got in beside him and handed him the money. 'There's not much damage. We've done what we came out for,' she said. 'Now, your place or mine?'

'If that was your father, we'd better make it mine.' He sounded relieved. She could guess that he had expected that the arrival of a father would have put a spoke in his wheel.

Eight

Celia's previous experiences of physical love had consisted of a few brief encounters, each little more than a thank-you for a pleasant evening, or a quick coupling, after protracted and unconventional foreplay, with Tasker O'Neill who thereafter preferred to sleep alone. It was a novel but not unpleasant experience to wake up with a man in the bed with her.

The night's passion had exceeded her most salacious dreams. Each had been delighted to discover a partner with precisely matching desires. They had writhed together in a glut of enjoyment but, in their tired state, they had each fallen into sleep as soon as their passion had been spent. She had woken once during the night, still entwined with his limbs and therefore much too hot, but she had managed to make a little space and fall asleep again.

She had expected their awakening to be a letdown but it was tender and wholesome. Ken was a clean person. He had shaved late the previous day so that stubble was not yet a problem. She was still deliciously sleepy and Ken, since he had been on duty until after midnight, would have been justified if he had lain in for another hour or two. But her conscience was pricking her. She began to slip quietly out of bed but a strong arm snaked around her and pulled her back.

'I thought you were still asleep,' she said.

'Well, I'm not.'

'I must go and let Dram out and give her some breakfast. Can I borrow your Land Rover?'

'Yes. Quite right, must always remember the dog. But not yet.' He pulled her to him. His energy amazed her. This time was even more delicious. There was no sleepiness, no embarrassment, no hesitation, just an impetuous expression of mutual delight.

While they were cooling and breathing he said, 'Will you be back? Or was this just a glorious one-night stand?'

'I was going to ask you the same thing,' she said. 'If you want me, I'll be back.'

'I expect to want you eternally. But you don't need my Land Rover. It's a long and hard way round by road but it's no distance by way of the fields. You'd be quicker walking and in no danger of being stopped by the police.'

'You don't mind my being seen coming out of your cottage?'

'God, no! I hope you'll be seen every day for years.'

So Celia resumed at least some of the clothes that she had worn the night before and walked, as directed, along a track beside a fence and through the corner of a wood. She followed a stream that turned out to be the feeder stream to the loch. The day had turned gloomy but she never noticed that the sun had stopped shining.

Dram emerged, stretching but looking no more than mildly curious, as Celia opened the door. Dram had become used to irregular comings and goings. Celia fed the spaniel. She had fallen into her father's habit of feeding twice a day on the grounds that a single larger meal stretched the stomach muscles. They walked back together with Dram hunting enthusiastically through the bushes. Celia had a proper look at the outside of the keeper's cottage for the first time as a prospective occupant. It seemed to be a cut above the average for such dwellings, being of good stonework and supporting several rather good rambling roses. The bargeboards and eaves were of fancy woodwork. She judged that it had probably been built to house some indigent female relative of an earlier laird.

Ken had already prepared a suitably nourishing breakfast for the humans. Celia, who had not eaten a proper meal for what seemed like days, waded into the bacon, eggs and pork sausages, with toast and coffee, and could not help making little noises of pleasure. Dram, who had inspected and approved the keeper's cottage, as she would have approved any dwelling containing her new mistress, curled up between her feet.

Ken, who had been unable to refrain from making a start to the meal, finished first. 'Now we talk about what comes next,' he said.

She emptied her mouth. 'Nothing really has to come next,' she said carefully. 'You don't owe me anything. Whatever comes, remember that you're not under any pressure.' She waited anxiously for his reaction.

'But I want something to come next.' Ken sounded both plaintive and indignant. 'I don't know what sort of blokes you've been with in the past, to give you the idea that all men want sex without commitment. I want a whole lot to come next. I want commitment. I want you to go on teaching me my job – I'm not too proud to learn from a woman! And as to what happened last night, I thought that I knew how wonderful it could be but I hadn't the beginning of an idea. I want it to happen over and over again.' He stumbled onward. 'I don't have a lot to offer you just at the moment; in fact, I'm just about broke. And I can't offer you marriage because we don't know whether my wife's alive or dead. But marriage should only be promising to do what you're going to do anyway. I want you to move in here.'

There was one acid test. 'How would you

feel about my having your babies?'

She watched him carefully but though he looked bashful he showed no sign of dismay. 'If you'd like to have my children, I'd be proud and happy.'

Celia, who had no hang-ups about orange blossom and bridal gowns, was sympathetic to his views and warmed by their sentiment. She gave him a look that was more meaningful than a mere kiss. 'How will the laird feel about you having a woman move in with you, knowing that you may still have a wife.'

'I'll have to find out. If he doesn't like it, we can go somewhere else.'

'Let's hope it doesn't come to that,' she said. 'You'd better ask him.' Her mind was putting aside the euphoria of sentiment and coming to grips with practicalities. 'At the same time, ask him if he'll pay for getting your Land Rover fixed. After all, it happened on the estate's business. It only needs a dent bashed out and a new sidelight. Better get it done straight away. I can give you the address of a man not too far away from here who fixes Land Rovers. He does a good job dirt-cheap. You should have change out of that hundred, but in case you don't I can give you some money. You'd better do some shopping.'

'I'm not totally broke yet,' he expostulated. 'When I am, I'll come to you. But you're right. We need bread, milk, meat—'

'We don't need to buy meat,' she said. 'Or fish. Nor vegetables, living as we do among fields of the stuff. But before you go, you have a job to do.' She produced a small bottle. 'Touch in my parting for me.'

'No trouble.' He smiled suddenly. 'I've just been swearing eternal love to you and I've just realized that I don't know your name.'

She broke into an enormous, involuntary grin. 'Just call me Lady Chatterley,' she said.

While she waited for her hair to dry, she renewed the spots and patches of dye on Dram's coat and then assessed her new abode. The cottage was slightly larger than the one by the loch, having a sitting room, a dining kitchen and two bedrooms. It was in need of decoration and the furnishing and carpets were overdue for renewal, but it was well equipped with a small freezer, a microwave and a washing machine as well as proper central heating (none of which were present in Loch Cottage).

Viewed from the windows, the cottage had a back garden that could certainly be productive, but it seemed to have been suffering from several years during which it had received attention only when a busy man could spare time for essential cultivation of foodstuffs. The result was a mass of weeds with patches of over-wintered vegetables or clean brown earth. Beyond the garden walls were fields and, never more than two fields away, trees. Most of the fields seemed to be in crop, but she could see cattle. Across a single field of barley was the cluster of farm buildings where they had collected the drum that was now in place at the new release pen and partly filled with grain. At the nearer side of a Dutch barn was what seemed to be a dumping-ground for whatever was not immediately needed. Tractor attachments lay beside a short row of black shapes that she knew would be straw or silage bales in polythene.

The cupboards were not well stocked. That at least was something that she could get on with while she waited for Ken's return. She called Dram to heel and set off back to the loch. She kept her eyes open for fields of edible vegetables. At the same time she was spying out a route from the loch to the keeper's cottage that could be accomplished on the scooter, passing gates rather than styles.

The cottage smelled sad, as though it knew that it was to be deserted again. She gathered her few odds and ends and those of Dram, restored things to how she remembered them and borrowed the fishing rod for what might well turn out to be the last time. Dram sat patiently while her mistress cast. It was not the ideal time of day. The sun, in its usual contrary way, had emerged again and was now too bright for easy fishing. No trout were rising but they would be feeding deep. One fish was feeding on terrestrial insects falling from an overhanging tree and she soon brought him out. Then she tied on a team of nymphs and fished deep under the edges of the weed.

With six good fish in the bag and the rabbits from the meat safe added, she wheeled out the scooter. Dram, to her relief, seemed happy to canter along level with her back wheel. Dram needed the exercise and Celia wanted to familiarize herself with the layout, so she rode around the estate roads, looking into release pens and coverts and making plans. She passed several small groups of two or three houses. She saw very few human figures but she knew that she was the object of curiosity. No doubt word had already gone round about a girl in the keeper's cottage.

Back at Ken's cottage, an exhausted Dram collapsed into her bed. There was no sign of Ken, but she would not have expected him back so soon. There was neither time nor money to begin decoration but at least she could start with a clean house. There was an apron in a kitchen drawer and a mop in a cupboard although neither seemed to have seen much recent service. She filled a bucket with hot soapy water and began on the kitchen. She had finished the floor and was beginning on the worktops when she heard a firm knock at the door.

She opened it, expecting the postman, but found a pleasant-faced, slightly plump woman a little older than herself. This lady wore a light summer print, which suggested that she had not come very far, and she was carrying a basket.

'Good morning,' Celia said. She looked down at her watch. It was a minute after noon. 'Or perhaps I should say "Good afternoon".'

The visitor had a pleasant smile and her teeth were good. 'An Australian would say "Good day" and not have to worry about it. I'm Margaret Gracie. My husband's the estate manager.'

'And he runs the shoot. Which, I suppose, makes him Ken's boss. Won't you come in?' Realizing that she was still wearing the apron she took it off and dropped it quickly on the hallstand.

'Thank you.' Mrs Gracie stepped over the threshold. 'I can see that I'm interrupting you at work. Do you mind?'

'Not in the least,' Celia said. 'Some jobs are better interrupted.'

Mrs Gracie nodded sympathetically. 'Any house that's been occupied by a solo man turns into an Augean stable, doesn't it.'

'Yes indeed. And my Hercules seems to be rather busier than just busy just now. But I've been looking forward to meeting neighbours.' As she spoke, she led the way into the sitting room. Celia was realizing that the time for introducing herself was nigh. She had told Ken her real name. If the police were hunting for her it would be in the name of Celia. 'I'm Joan Lightfoot.'

'Joan. Please call me Margaret.'

They stumbled through the usual preliminaries. Margaret Gracie declined coffee. They agreed that the day had begun badly but was now more like what they were entitled to expect at that time of year. They enquired about children – neither had any.

Margaret soon came to the point. 'The signs are that you may be moving in with Kenny.'

'It does seem a bit that way.'

'Sam Smith – that's the younger of the two men who helped you yesterday – said that you seemed to be a couple. And I saw you leaving here this morning. Ken isn't the sort of man for what they call one-night stands.'

'And you don't want to see him hurt?'

'That's very perceptive of you. That's exactly what I was going to say.'

Celia – or Joan – had had time to consider how she would express herself to neighbours. The time for openness seemed to have arrived. 'Margaret, perhaps it will save embarrassment if I say that I do know about Ken's wife. He doesn't know what happened to her and I've made it clear to him that if she comes back again I'll move out, pronto.'

Margaret leaned forward and looked into her eyes. 'My dear, if she's alive, I don't think she'll come back. She hated being a keeper's wife. I think she found somebody with better prospects. And if she did return I doubt if Kenny would have her back. She behaved very badly towards him.'

Joan – perhaps the time has come for us to call her by her true name – had no desire to talk about Ken's wife. She seemed to be a sore subject with him and some of that soreness had transferred itself to Joan. In search of another topic she said, 'Tell me about Sam Smith.'

Margaret shrugged. 'There's nothing much to tell. He lived with his mother in one of the cottages beyond the farmhouse where we live. You can see our roof from here, diagonally across the field. He was a bit of a mother's boy. He did leave once to set up his own business but I think it failed. Anyway, his mother had a stroke and he came back to look after her. She died last month. I doubt if he'll stay long.'

'And the older man? Who was he?'

'I believe his name's Jeremiah, which suits him rather well. They call him Gerry. If he has another name I never heard it. He's a miserable old so-and-so. He lives with his wife and they fight like cat and dog. They seem to enjoy it. Will Ken be back soon?'

'I don't know,' Joan said. 'We caught a poacher last night and the Land Rover was slightly damaged. He's away getting it fixed.'

Margaret produced a generous smile. 'So that's why you were so late! We heard the Land Rover come back and thought you might have been whooping it up in Newton Lauder.'

Joan had a sudden onset of comprehension. 'And your husband sent you along to find out what sort of woman had got her claws into Ken. Yes?'

'You've got it. I'll report that Kenny has landed himself a much more suitable woman and that we can look forward to a little more stability in the keepering department. Oh, and I brought you a little welcoming present. A date and walnut cake.'

'My favourite!' Joan exclaimed.

'My own baking. We'll see if it's still your favourite after you've eaten it.' Margaret showed signs of leaving, but Joan recognized a Heaven-sent source of local information. For a few minutes Margaret was persuaded to touch on the local personalities. 'I must be going now,' she said at last. 'Next time I'll phone first and if you're still cleaning the Augean stable I'll wear something older and give you a hand.'

'If you do, I'll probably do a sacrifice in your honour. Before you go, one last question. Can you tell me who owns this furniture?'

Margaret looked around sympathetically. 'It's pretty far gone, isn't it. I'm sure it doesn't belong to the estate. If it isn't Kenny's, it must have belonged to Jim McKee. I can't say that I'm surprised he left it behind.'

Celia – or Joan as we must now call her – had almost finished the kitchen when the telephone rang. Ken was on the line. 'I'll be a little late,' he said, 'but I'll be starting back soon. Your pal's prices are pretty good, as you said. There were several things needed on the Land Rover—'

'You don't have to explain,' Joan said. 'Come when you can. Trout for tea.'

She finished cleaning the kitchen and made a toasted cheese sandwich for her lunch. She was contemplating a serious attack on the bathroom when the doorknocker clattered again. This time the figure on the doorstep was male, fortyish, lean but muscular and as bald as an egg. He had a moustache that Joan could only think of as military. He wore clean corduroys below his green quilted jacket. She was grateful that she had at least tidied her hair before sitting down to her lunch.

'Good afternoon. Miss Lightfoot? I'm Harold Gracie, the estate manager. May I come in?'

'Ken isn't here at the moment. He's having the Land Rover fixed. It was damaged by a poacher last night.'

'That's all right. It was you that I wanted to see.'

'And I very much wanted to see you,' she said. She led the way into the sitting room and indicated a chair. 'You go first.'

'Very well.' He put the tips of his fingers together. 'Let's be blunt. Will you be around for long?'

It deserved an answer. 'I hope so,' she said. 'Ken and I only met recently but we were immediately *simpatico*. He's in a difficult position, not knowing whether his wife is alive or dead, but we seem to be agreed that we'll marry as soon as we can. I told him that if his wife returns I'll move out.'

'Margaret told me. She says that she told you that Whetstone wouldn't want that. She's probably right. She very often is, especially about that sort of thing. To be frank, she was quite the wrong sort of wife for him. Or for anybody else,' he added after a moment's thought. 'But the reason for my question is this. Kenny seems to have been making heavy weather of the job.'

Joan felt her hackles rising. The statement was absolutely true but she resented it on Ken's behalf. 'He has a great deal of theoretical knowledge. He took the assistant keeper's job to learn the practicalities and he has been treated very badly.'

Mr Gracie stiffened. 'In what way?'

'In almost every way. Jim McKee gave him no instruction, just used him for the donkeywork. Nobody even told him that the syndicate members were supposed to pitch in and help with all the work. And Mr McKee clung on to all the tips so that Kenny was left without more than two pennies to rub together.'

Mr Gracie tried to hide his look of discomfort. 'I didn't know that.'

'It's a bit late to find out now. Wouldn't it be part of your job to see that the estate's employees were in a position to survive? But there's a long wait until next season. You see the state of this place? Apparently it's left to Ken to replace the furnishings, but if you pay him a pauper's wage and don't make the tips good, he won't be able to buy proper furniture.'

She left the words *and I won't stick around* hanging in the air between them.

Mr Gracie pursed his lips. 'I'll be honest with you,' he said. 'We were on the point of bringing in an expert to sort things out. Ken would have had to go. But I've just been round the shoot. The last couple of days have seen a transformation. That seems to be down to you. Whether it's a matter of morale or of expertise or another pair of hands I wouldn't know—'

'My father was a gamekeeper.' This was true as far as it went. 'That's another point. Ken's entitled to an under-keeper.'

'Would you take the job on?'

'Not at the wages you were paying him.'

Mr Gracie shied away from the subject of money. 'I can call round the members and arrange a working party for this weekend. And there's some refurbishment due at the big house. The drawing-room carpet's going out and the suite. They're in reasonable condition. If I had them cleaned and steered them your way ... '

'I'm so glad to find you so reasonable,' Joan said. She smiled as sweetly as she could manage. 'May I take these things as definite?'

'Yes. I suppose so.'

'That's fine. And the garden has been neglected for years. With Ken so busy, I don't see him having time to do anything about it until next year. On the other hand, there's usually a quiet time in the farming calendar about now. Could we borrow Sam Smith to dig it over?'

'I ... I'll think about it.'

'That's splendid.' Joan had got the measure of Mr Gracie. 'It's so much better to thrash these things out between reasonable people than in front of an employment tribunal, don't you think? Now, hold on while I find a pencil and paper and we'll work out what would be a living wage for each of us between now and the first shoot of the season.'

Mr Gracie came out in a cold sweat. Joan was in no doubt that he had been skimming a little cream off the top, and an employment tribunal would ask all sorts of nasty questions about stamps, PAYE and the minimum wage. 'I suppose so,' he said.

The vixen had another body blow for him. 'Backdated,' she said.

Mr Gracie choked. His attempts to dominate the ensuing discussion were hampered by the way his eyes were watering.

Nine

Ken Whetstone returned home to find that his life would never be the same again. Instead, it had taken a considerable turn for the better. He had been granted a substantial pay increase backdated for some months, for renegotiation during the following October when the visitors' tips began to trickle in again. He also had a very competent assistant in Joan, who was also drawing a wage. And these were not the only signs that the person he had agreed to share his life with was a very forceful lady indeed. He found himself swept up into a whirlwind of organized effort.

The two immediately undertook another tour of the estate, listing the jobs that would be required of the working party to make all ready for the delivery of the poults, and then checked to be sure that the necessary tools and materials were available. Then, while Joan prepared the evening meal, Ken was set to choosing colours (subject to her approval) and estimating quantities of paint and paper for the whole cottage. Joan dug into her ill-gotten hoard to finance the immediate purchases.

The brief interim before the six-week-old birds arrived was devoted to a blitz on predators. About raptors they had largely to rely on the mirrors on the roofs of the shelters, but those would have little effect when the pheasant poults began to spread out. Joan explored the accumulated gear in the sheds and found among the pigeon decoys some rubber crows (used as confidence decoys). These she placed near the two sites where sparrowhawks were nesting. Crows are persistent thieves of other birds' eggs and chicks. One sparrowhawk deserted immediately. The other was more determined, but Joan pointed out to Ken that 'It would be against nature to leave her nest on the side away from the crow. If she goes towards the crow she'll also be going away from our pen and towards the starlings. She's welcome to help herself to a few of them.'

They decimated the small local population of hooded crows with the air rifle and set traps and snares for ground predators. The pair spent several nights out with a lamp and rifle and accounted for two vixens which otherwise would soon have been feeding litters with the easiest prey available, which would be young pheasants. Ken proved to be a competent shot with the estate's .223 rifle but Joan had to teach him the difference in colour between a fox's eyes and those of a sheep, seen in the glare of the lamp. Later, when the remaining sparrowhawk turned its attention to young pheasants again, Joan fashioned a scarecrow, dressed in some outworn clothes begged from the farm workers, and posed it in realistic positions, lurking with what seemed to be a shotgun.

On the day of the working party there was a good turnout of members, including one doctor, three shopkeepers, a lorry driver, a retired policeman, a farmer, a civil servant and a very masculine lady who did the work of two. A present but less energetic member was the antiques dealer J. D. Farrow. Joan had to remind herself that although she had seen his face he had not seen hers.

By the end of the day all the pens were secure and protected by electric wires. Paths and sunning places had been cut through the weeds, perches had been provided to encourage the birds to learn to go up to roost, the feeders and drinkers and the drums containing fresh supplies were full and each release pen had been searched with care to ensure that when the doors were closed they would not be shutting any foxes or other predators inside with the pheasant poults.

Dram proved popular but attracted some curious glances. She also avoided Mr Farrow and hid behind Joan's legs at first whenever the antiques dealer was nearby. That behaviour might have started bells ringing, so Joan kept her confined in the cab of the Land Rover. Joan overheard one of the members ask Mr Farrow, 'Your Pam never turned up again?'

'No, never,' said Farrow. 'Somebody must have taken her in. Or maybe she got herself run over. Brutus is pining.'

Joan sneered into a bag of wheat. Brutus was certainly not pining.

'You should have had her microchipped,' said the other member. The remark was met with sullen silence. In hindsight, it was obvious.

Joan sighed with satisfaction on learning that Dram was not chipped. That she had lived in the company of the un-neutered Brutus suggested that she had been spayed. Joan's pleasure was increased when she heard another member, well out of earshot of Mr Farrow, remark, 'The poor bitch is better away from him. You'd think that handling antiques would have taught him the virtue of being gentle. I just hope that she's been taken in by somebody who knows how to treat a dog with respect.'

Four syndicate members promised to turn up when the birds were delivered, and two actually did so. By arrangement, the birds were delivered with wings already clipped. They were counted out into the widely scattered pens and watched to be sure that there was no immediate feather-picking or predation.

One job remained. On Joan's instructions, Ken had collected some dead hens from a nearby poultry farm. Each was poured full of antifreeze by way of a funnel and then hung on the wire of a pen. Sure enough, next morning two of the pens each had a dead vixen lying nearby. Joan picked them up with satisfaction as she set Ken to burying them. She missed the sight and sound of the hunt and knew that a pack of foxhounds was the one method of control that guaranteed a quick death for the fox or a total escape, but while poisoning with antifreeze remained legal and the hunt was not, poison it would have to be.

Then began the long summer's work. Predators had to be deterred, food and water carried, batteries charged, returned and reconnected. Young pheasants were soon finding their way out through the fox-proof pop-holes and had to be shepherded home at night.

It was a hard and tiring life for two, but Joan insisted on one rule. Between the evening meal and bed, unless Ken had to go out again, the two would devote an hour, no more and no less, to fixing up the cottage. Room by room, this became a small-scale version of the home that Joan had always wanted. The drawing-room carpet from the big house had suffered wear near the door and in front of the fireplace but the remainder was almost unmarked and large enough to cover most of the floors in the cottage.

To add to the workload, Simon Watson MP had purchased a part-trained Labrador bitch. In his book, keepers doubled as dog-trainers. Ken had little experience of dogs and none of their training, so this duty fell on Joan's shoulder. If two bitches share a home and dislike each other, the fur may fly. Happily Tanya and Dram got on well together. Tanya had a soft mouth and a friendly nature. She was soon familiar with all the commands and duties appropriate to a Labrador, except that she was impetuous. Rather than saddle the laird with a chronic runner-in, Joan spent hours tempting Tanya with dummies thrown nearby and checking firmly any tendency to move.

As summer advanced the young pheasants, growing larger and more adventurous, were tempted to wander and the presence of a second dog for 'dogging-in' the boundaries was a boon.

Ken was becoming more confident in his job every day. When he finally gained the confidence to give her an order, as keeper to assistant, Joan had to blink away tears of delight. He was never too proud to ask her advice and the intricacies of farming remained a mystery to him.

Late in the summer, when the shooting season was beginning to loom, Ken was already thinking towards the next spring. He pulled up the Land Rover at the gable of the Dutch barn and they got out. The cornfield was being harvested. A contracted combine harvester was making large round straw bales and a baler, owned by the estate, was following on, picking up each bale without apparent effort and juggling it through a complex dance while the bale wrapped itself in black polythene. Thus the row of three black bales remaining from the previous autumn was growing ever longer again.

'I was thinking,' Ken said. 'I was reading somewhere that feeding the pheasants in a straw ride keeps them scratching for the grain. It's more natural, they don't have time to wander off and they're too busy to feather-pick. Could I get some of these bales, do you think? Are they heavy?'

'Not if they're kept dry. You'd have to ask Mr Gracie.'

'What do they use them for, anyway?'

The couple had come to a halt at the end of the row, looking across the field to where the keeper's cottage drowsed under the sun. 'They're used for cattle feed,' Joan said.

'Straw?' He sounded incredulous.

'About January or February, when the cows have calved and need nutrition but there isn't the grass any more, the straw gets chopped up and mixed with molasses to feed them.' Mention of cows calving brought fecundity back to her mind. As a conscious decision, she had stopped taking any precautions against pregnancy. She wondered again what would be the consequences if she had a son by Ken. She was in no position to invite the welfare state to support her. Ken, she was sure, would stand by her. Unless ... 'Ken,' she said, 'is your wife ever coming back?'

Ken made a sound suggesting that he had trodden in something nasty. 'I doubt it very much. Very much indeed. It's almost exactly a year now and she's probably forgotten that this place exists. She never put down roots here. Even if she's deserted some lover, I don't think that this is where she'd come back to. As a matter of fact, the longer she stays away the more her few good points seem to fade away and the clearer her faults become in my memory. It just wouldn't be in her nature to leave one man until she'd lined up the next one, I see that now.'

'But you think she's still alive?'

Joan studied Ken fondly as he considered the question. He had filled out, with the physical work allied to the wholesome food. He had a tan and his nose was peeling. She decided to warn him to wear a hat rather than suffer ageing or skin cancer. 'On the whole I doubt it,' he said at last. 'I can't believe that she'd run off without a triumphant last word. And she took none of her clothes, except what I suppose she stood up in, although she set great store by some of them. They're still in the spare room. You may as well get the use of them.'

Joan jumped back like a startled horse. 'Christ, no!' she said. 'You probably wouldn't notice if a dress you'd seen on one woman turned up on another, but you're a man. A woman would spot it immediately. If people around here saw me in what they recognized as her clothes, what would they think? Would they decide that we knew she wasn't coming back?' The questions were rhetorical. Rather than wait for an answer she moved on. 'Do you think that somebody killed her?'

His face froze for a moment. 'If you force me to consider it,' he said, 'yes I do. Now that I've had time to think about her without being confused by her presence, I can see that she was exactly the type to get murdered. Promiscuous, ruthless, totally self-centred, clinging, sexually both clever and demanding.'

'Then where's her body?' She saw him flinch. 'I'm not for a moment suggesting that you have guilty knowledge,' she said, half laughing. 'I'm just speculating where around here one could hide a body.'

He relaxed and leaned back against the end bale. The shadows of the trees were beginning to stretch across the stubble. In the soft light the distant hills looked closer. 'She needn't be around here at all,' he said. 'She could have been picked up by a lover and carried a hundred miles away, then been killed and disposed of.'

Once having embarked on the line of thought, Joan's mind was searching around, indoors and out, in search of inspiration. 'Yes, but disposed of how?'

'Think of the ways that have been used. Deaths have been disguised as suicide, a natural death or an accident. Killers have used acid baths. Cremation. In water. Buried deep. Fed to animals. Or bodies have been left for the police to examine, but with all identity removed ... '

Joan shivered. 'That,' she said, 'is very much more than quite enough.' All the same, curiosity drove her on. 'If you were stuck with a body, mine if you like—'

'Dear God no!' he said.

'Thank you for that. Then let's suppose that it's somebody you didn't like very much. How would you get rid of it?'

'There was a man once,' he said slowly. 'Or maybe there were hundreds of men but the others all got away with it. He kept the body in a deep freeze until it was frozen solid. Then he hired a wood chipper, towed it at night to a bridge miles from anywhere and fed the body through the chipper. The chipped bits sprayed down into the river and the fishes did the rest. It was all gone by morning. With the Land Rover, I think I could tow a wood chipper down to the loch.'

'I was going to give you trout for your tea,' Joan said. She could feel her lip curling.

'Let's have wood-pigeon breasts,' he said. 'We can have trout tomorrow. Anyway, our freezer wouldn't hold more than part of a leg.'

'Not even that,' she said. 'It's full of venison and trout and that half-pig you bought off old Simpson.'

'When the tips start coming in, we'll have to think about a larger freezer.'

Joan nodded happily. He was beginning to get his priorities right.

Ten

During the early summer, very little had been seen of Simon Watson MP. Most of his time was spent at Westminster and when he managed a period at home he was committed to surgeries in his constituency office a few miles away. He was a Liberal Democrat and his reputation was as a conscientious and hardworking MP.

When Westminster took its summer recess, however, Mr Watson vanished and was understood to be holidaying abroad. On his return, though he hurried to catch up with constituency business, he had time for more personal interests. Word came back to Ken and Joan that he had been inspecting the pheasants in and out of their release pens. He called at the cottage, they were told, but at a time when they were both out around the feeders and traps. Joan saw him at a distance that evening, shooting pigeon as they came in to roost in a tree strip well away from the pheasant coverts. She judged that he was a very competent shot.

It was one of those perfect evenings that had proved to be rather rare that year. The earlier breeze had dropped, the sky seemed to go on forever and the evening light glowed rosily over all. Between shots, the silence was so total that the sound of an incoming pigeon was clearly audible. She hurried home and collected Tanya. Experience suggested that the midges would be out in their millions so she anointed her neck and ears with insect repellent.

Mr Watson had tucked himself into the concealment of three alder trees. She made sure that he had seen her and then began working Tanya from a position within a nearby hedge, to the annoyance of a blackbird nesting nearby. When the light was going and the supply of pigeon dried up, she introduced herself to the dark shape that was her employer.

'I intended to come and meet you,' he said. 'Would tomorrow morning suit? And is this the bitch you're training for me?'

'Yes, this is Tanya. Tomorrow morning will be fine. Do you want Ken Whetstone to be there?'

'No. I don't think that will be necessary, I

already know him. But have him there if you want him.'

'I'll see how he feels about it,' Joan said. Would having Ken present make it seem that she suspected Mr Watson of improper intentions? Or would meeting Mr Watson alone suggest that she was open to any such an approach? She decided that she had said enough for the moment. 'Tanya's coming on well. You still have two birds to pick, maybe more. Would you like to work her?'

'I would indeed. It isn't too soon?'

'Not a bit,' she said. 'One dropped at the foot of that tall pine. Tell her to "Fetch" while you direct her that way. You'll see.'

Even in near-darkness, Tanya performed perfectly. The laird was properly impressed. At the end, however, he was still sure that one bird was missing. 'We've given it a good search,' Joan said. 'If Tanya can't find it, either it's a strong runner or it's caught up in a tree. I'll look for it in the morning.' (Or, she thought, you only imagined you hit it.)

The laird had nineteen birds in the bag. 'Would you like to have these?' he asked. 'My housekeeper gets very uptight if she's asked to prepare and cook anything that didn't come across a shop counter.'

'Thank you. And I'll wait in for you in the

morning. Shall I take your gun and clean it? That's usually part of a keeper's duties.'

'Don't bother. I'll be down by eleven tomorrow. Good night.'

Joan hurried home and hung her pigeon in the larder. She decided that she had liked his voice. She had held his gun for him while he took a pigeon from Tanya and she could tell by the balance and by the porcelain finish of the stock that it was a gun of top quality.

In the morning, she took both dogs out and found the missing bird stuck in the branches of a spruce tree. She was back in plenty of time to be ready for Mr Watson. She cut the breasts out of the pigeon and bagged the remainder for disposal. She had not made an effort beyond a wash and brush, the removal of any loose pigeon feathers and the preparation of coffee. There was not going to be any forelock-tugging, she had decided. And if he wished to be addressed as sir, he would have to earn the privilege.

He arrived, on foot, a minute or two after eleven. She took him into the sitting room. He accepted coffee. He was a sandy-haired man, nearing sixty, with pale blue eyes that protruded slightly and uneven teeth. His suit had been cut to hide the beginning of a belly. She gave him full marks for keeping it informal, as between colleagues rather than laird to serf.

'I wanted to see you,' he said, 'with or without your – um – Mr Whetstone. Perhaps it's easier without him. From what I hear, he grew into the job rather suddenly. General opinion is that this was your doing.'

'Ken knows a great deal of theory,' she said firmly. 'As the daughter of a former keeper, I know the practicalities. We are learning from each other.'

'And a very good relationship you seem to have established. The season will be on us before very much longer. Will you still be with us?'

'I hope so,' she said stiffly. 'We're assuming so. Ken and I have already considered how we will organize a day. We thought that Ken would control the beating line and I would stay with the Guns. That means that I would give the usual talk about safety. I trust that I would have your support?'

It was evident from his expression that he had been thinking along quite other lines. 'Yes, of course,' he said vaguely. 'I think that that's a very sensible plan. But what I was really asking was whether you, personally, were here to stay.'

'Perhaps you should ask Ken.'

He saw that she was amused and he gave a short laugh. 'Yes, I do sound a little like a heavy father. Perhaps I should be asking him whether his intentions are honourable. We have eleven days booked this season so far and probably more to come. If you were to decide that this life wasn't for you, could he manage without you?'

She had a momentary surge of anger but before she could retort she realized that his question was reasonable. He would have committed himself to commercial bookings. He would have issued invitations, some of them to political or business contacts. Bad or cancelled days could leave him with egg all over his face.

'I would not make such a decision,' she said. 'I feel happier and more settled here than ever before in my life. Mr Whetstone and I hope to get married when we can, but as long as his wife remains beyond reach we can't. Eventually, if she never turns up at all, he may be able to ask the courts to declare her dead. But the only thing that could damage this relationship would be if she were to come back and fight a divorce – in which case he would expect you to provide him with an assistant and I would certainly apply for the job. But that seems very unlikely. For now, we're quite prepared to go on as we are and in this day and age it's nobody's business but our own.'

'That,' he said, 'may not be entirely true. I won my seat in Parliament, at least in part, by arguing for the return of family values. In the event of a scandal, I might have to consider your position. You might be well advised not to flaunt any closer relationship than keeper and assistant who happen to share a house. But you could let it be known that you intend to marry if circumstances permit.'

He seemed to be suggesting that she walk two simultaneous and possibly divergent tightropes. 'Do you think it likely,' she asked, 'that circumstances will ever permit?'

He pursed his lips. He was looking down at the carpet as though wondering where he had seen it before. 'I suppose it's inevitable that you would want to know. If you want my opinion, and strictly between ourselves, I doubt it. I knew Mrs Whetstone. Oh, not in the biblical sense,' he said quickly, 'though that was always on the cards. My wife was killed in a car accident five years ago and I'm not so old as to have outgrown those sort of needs, but it would have been a great mistake to get too intimate with the wife of an employee.' (Joan noted the sentiment. *So I needn't worry*, she thought. She must have let the thought show because he smiled for an instant.) 'I met her about the place now and again, that much was inevitable, and we indulged in a little flirtation at a harmless level. I'm sure you know the sort of thing – little double entendres with a sidelong glance. A fluttering of her eyelashes. Not intended to be taken seriously. She may have taken it more seriously than I did, although I doubt it. But I knew, everybody knew, that she had a definitely roving eye. It was either common knowledge or an ugly rumour – it can be very difficult sometimes to separate the two – that when she went to another house to cook or clean she would allow the man of the house certain favours and expect to be rewarded for them. She was a common little piece but very attractive in an aggressive way and she knew how to make the most of herself.'

As he spoke, his use of the past tense had become obvious. 'What do you think became of her?' Joan asked.

His eyebrows shot up. 'It's hardly for me to have an opinion,' he said.

'Perhaps not,' Joan said. 'But it has a bearing on what you mentioned earlier, the possibility of scandal.'

'I suppose that's so. If she's still alive, she could come back and make a scene, even make a fuss in the papers. But I don't think it's likely.

'The day that she vanished I met her in mid-afternoon. She was cycling up the drive but she stopped beside the water tower to speak with me. There was a new joy in her face and a light in her eye. She said that she was leaving her husband because she had had a better offer. I thought, frankly, that it was a hell of a thing to say, but I had a feeling that she had made up her mind to a total change in her lifestyle and that she was throwing aside all the preconceptions of behaviour.

'The last thing I wanted was a lot of domestic disruption among the staff, so I asked her if she was really sure. She must have misunderstood me. She said that there was still time for that offer to be gazumped. I'm not making this up,' Mr Watson said plaintively. 'Those were her words.

'Her meaning was plain and it was reinforced by her manner. Whoever her lover was, I would be a better proposition and she would change her loyalties like a shot, given a little encouragement. Nothing was said about marriage, but in my position living openly with a mistress would spell disaster. It seemed tactful to suggest that my affections were engaged elsewhere.'

Joan managed not to ask whether there had been any truth in the statement. 'Thank you for telling me. I'll respect your confidence,' she said.

'Thank you. But you see why I wouldn't expect her to return here. She was on the lookout for the best prospect and even if she had fallen out with her lover of the time, a gamekeeper would have come low on the list.' He paused and looked around the room more carefully. In decorating, Joan had been tempted to make use of her favourite blue, but the room might be cold and dull in winter. In the hope of luring in a little sunshine she had chosen a creamy yellow for three walls and the ceiling with the fourth wall a purple brown. The contrast, set off by the plum carpet and the colours in the print that covered the suite, harmonized surprisingly well. 'You might be well advised to not turn the keeper's cottage into too much of a showplace,' he said, smiling. 'In my opinion, that's the one thing that might tempt her into making a return. I want to freshen up some more of my house. Would you care to give me your advice on colours?'

'I'd be delighted. When you met her, was anything said about who, when and how?'

'*Who* would probably be somebody fairly local. She lived a circumscribed life here and would hardly ever meet a stranger except when she went into Newton Lauder to earn some extra money. By the time Parliament next went into recess it was old news anyway. That's when I discovered that she was not living with anybody local. By then, she could easily have gone off with a local on a trip abroad and met somebody else. She was a flighty piece.

'As to *when* and *how*, I had the impression that she was expecting to be picked up on the main road fairly soon and had only come back to pack a few things.'

'Nearly all her *things* are still in the cottage,' Joan said.

Mr Watson looked concerned but he managed to shrug. 'She could have found herself short of time and decided to abandon them, knowing that her lover was more than capable of replacing them.'

'I suppose it's possible. The alternative is that she's dead.'

Mr Watson's bland face produced a ferocious scowl. He lowered his voice. 'Don't say that. Don't even think it. This could be just the sort of scandal that my enemies are waiting to pounce on.'

It was Joan's belief that, politically, Simon Watson was not a significant enough figure to have enemies. Rivals, perhaps. 'I suppose,' she said, 'that almost any man around here could be thought to have a motive. But don't worry too much about it. If that's what happened, she could have been taken away by car. Her lover could have discovered that she wasn't God's gift to his libido after all and killed and buried her at the other end of the country.' It felt strange to be trying to reassure a Member of Parliament, but she had become quite accustomed to calming any self-doubt on Ken's part.

Evidently she had started Mr Watson's mind working. 'It could be said that you had as good a motive as anybody,' he pointed out.

'Yes. Except that I can prove that I never met Ken until long after she disappeared.' *But God forbid that I should have to*, she thought.

'Count yourself lucky. With a little more luck she may never surface again.'

'In which case it may be years before Ken

and I can marry.'

'According to recent statistics, more babies are born out of wedlock than within it.'

This seemed to Joan to be the usual specious argument of a politician as well as being a U-turn. She was fairly sure that the statistics proved only that more couples co-habited without being married than otherwise, which in turn suggested that many dashed to the altar, or at least the registry office, as soon as a family began to loom up.

She was getting tired of the subject of Mrs Whetstone, and anyway they did not have enough data to sustain a reasoned discussion. 'Coming back to the day of the shoot,' she said, 'who pays the beaters?'

They settled down to a detailed discussion of duties and responsibilities.

Eleven

The first shoot was held early in October, on a day that was cooler but still fine and sunny. The legal season for pheasants lasts for only four months, but bearing in mind that they are not usually fully mature for the first month, the season may usually be regarded as lasting a mere three months. To make fullest use of the season and to catch the best of the weather, Mr Watson and Mr Gracie had agreed that a corner of the estate should be given over to ex-laying hen pheasants, thus providing good adult birds early in the season. This was the only corner of the estate that would be shot that day. The two shoots in October would thin the birds out and when they were past the year's poults would be ready to spread out and fill the gaps.

Dawn still arrives early at the beginning of October. Ex-laying hen pheasants, having known other territories, are less habituated to thinking of a particular place as 'home' and so are more inclined to wander off. Joan and Ken were out early, 'dogging-in' the boundaries to turn back any wanderers. In the process they checked that the wind was from its due quarter and that the numbered pegs at each drive were still upright and in positions which experience and hunch suggested would put them under the birds.

They returned to the cottage for a good breakfast and then, while Ken went to check again that all the gear was ready, Joan began an extra task that usually falls to the keeper's wife – preparing lunch for the beaters. This was to be a shoot that the laird was saving for himself and his guests, so a proper team of beaters had been made up by borrowing from the Ilwand estate next door. A beating team may be made up without reference to the usual loyalties, so most of the faces were familiar, some belonging to the Watson estate and others to casual workers accustomed to working for any employer needing their skills at the time. The rewards for struggling through the prickly cover were slight – a small sum of money and a pheasant or two – so most were there for the pleasure of a day in the country and the company of like-minded souls.

The Guns were assembling at the big house, but the beaters and pickers-up were to meet at the keeper's cottage. Ken was already experienced in controlling the beaters' line, a task to which he had been relegated while Jim McKee took on the more remunerative job of attending on the Guns. Ken and Joan had duplicate copies of maps with the day's drives marked on. He was to keep and work Dram the spaniel. Joan set off with Tanya the labrador at heel, muttering over and over her own words for the customary instructions to the Guns.

She found the guests with their host starting the day with Buck's Fizz on the gravel sweep in front of the big house. She watched carefully to see that none was over-indulging. Dogs seemed to be everywhere. She had agreed with the MP that she would be introduced as Miss Lightfoot, the assistant keeper. During the introductions, she was startled to find herself face to face with Mr Farrow, the amorous antiques dealer who had unwittingly furnished most of her survival funds. She knew that he was a member of the syndicate but she had not realized that he was a friend of the laird. She reminded herself again that although she had seen enough of his face to recognize him he had not seen hers before the working party.

Among her duties was the taking of entries for sweepstakes on the day's bag and on the gun to bring down the first pheasant. Other duties included organizing the draw for peg positions and dispensing cartridges from the back of the laird's Range Rover.

Simon Watson called for a hush and nodded to her. She began with a huskiness that soon cleared. 'If you have the chance of a safe shot at a fox,' she said, 'take it, but be sure that the shot is perfectly safe. No other ground game at all, ever. Keep dogs strictly beside you; if you decide to send your dog after a runner, make sure that the nearest picker-up knows and agrees. All the other rules are common sense. Don't move away from your peg. A horn will mark the start of a drive and another horn the finish, after which no more shots, please. Make yourself aware of the positions of your neighbours and of any picker-up behind you. Crossing an obstacle, please hand your gun, open and empty, to somebody else and, similarly, when walking to and from your peg, open and empty, please.'

'Not bagged?' enquired a voice.

'Bagged if you like, but I prefer to be able

to see that the gun is unloaded.' (There was a mutter of agreement.) 'Finally, please be sensible at all times. If you are turning to take a bird behind you, unmount the gun, raise the barrels while you turn and then mount the gun again. Unless you can see clear sky or empty landscape beyond with a good margin round about, do not fire. Any dangerous behaviour will result in the culprit being sent to sit in his car. I believe that I have a promise of Mr Watson's support in this.'

Simon Watson hesitated for a second before saying, 'Definitely!'

'You have your peg numbers. At each drive, move up three. On that note,' Joan said, *'Wagons roll!'*

There was a little friendly laughter as Guns and dogs sorted themselves into vehicles. Space in four-by-fours was found for those whose cars were unsuited to rough going.

By arrangement, Joan joined Simon Watson at his Range Rover. 'You drive,' he said. 'I may want to send you somewhere in the Range Rover and this is a good chance to judge your competence.'

The laird's car was to lead the way. At least Joan knew the roads and tracks well enough.

Once she had mastered the gears and the unfamiliar feel of the clutch and other controls, she managed well. 'Did I do the talk all right?' she asked.

'Did I interrupt you?'

'No.'

'Then you did all right.' There was a smile in his voice.

They went by way of single-track roads with passing places and took to a farm track down to a strip of grass below a wooded hillside. Vehicles were parked to one side and the Guns sought their pegs. Some, of course, had already forgotten their numbers. There were three other pickers-up and Joan placed them carefully, reserving for herself a position where she thought the action might be hottest.

A horn sounded in the distance. There was a quickening of interest. Breath came faster. They had waited for this moment and now skill would be put to the test. While the tapping of the beaters' sticks and their dog-whistles were still a long way off, a well-grown hen appeared suddenly over the trees on the hill. Having started from high ground and then climbed to clear the trees, it was a very high bird indeed, slanting at high speed down the hillside in front of the Guns. There was a popping as four Guns in succession had a try. Suddenly the bird's head went back, she rolled over and dropped as an inanimate ball of meat and feathers. Joan held on to the memory.

The beaters were performing well. There were rarely more than four birds at a time in the air and not often less. The steady trickle was just as it should be. Joan noted the reliability of the Guns. Several could be counted for a clean kill with almost every shot. One never touched a feather, and this she found quite acceptable. The birds would be there for next time. More of a worry were two who regularly wounded their birds. Tanya, also, was acquitting herself well. This was her first venture from training to the real objective, a stage at which a dog may break down, but she sat steady and unworried beside Joan, not moving until sent. They watched and memorized. There was no feeling of triumph at the kill; just satisfaction of a job done with skill and a worthy opponent beaten.

The horn went for the end of the drive. The pickup began in an orderly manner although there was an immediate dispute between two Guns, each wishing to claim the first bird. They turned to her for a decision. 'I was watching carefully,' she said. She tapped the shoulder of a man in green tweed. 'The shot was yours.' She was surprised to find that she was awarding the kitty to J. D. Farrow.

The pickup was made more difficult by the dog of one of the guests. Allowed to join in by kind permission of one of the pickers-up, it rushed to collect the bird, dropped it in order to go for another one and soon had all the dogs confused and competing. Joan got hold of its owner and told him to keep the dog on a lead in future until given her personal permission.

The game-cart arrived, a trailer behind a tractor driven by Sam Smith. Joan did not wait to watch the birds being hung carefully on the rack. Simon Watson was dispensing drinks from the back of his Range Rover. She caught his eye and gave a warning shake of the head. She was pleased to see that he reduced the strength of the drinks. When she had him to herself she said, 'If you get them all pissed, you'll find yourself running this shoot on your own.'

He looked like thunder for a second and she wondered if, like her father, she had gone too far. Perhaps she should have worded it more tactfully, but a tentative approach now might result in a tentative attitude to all safety issues. The MP hesitated and then nodded. 'Point taken. Safety is your responsibility and I can't fault you for insisting on it. We don't want any accidents. You drive again.'

At one time, Joan had stood in for the instructor at a clay-pigeon club. When they were back on the road and driving under a tunnel of beech trees in all their autumn glory she said, 'Two of your guests are mediocre shots. I don't mind them missing clean, but they're not killing clean. It's just not ethical to accept unnecessary wounding. The very tall chap with the deerstalker hat – Mr Bell, was it? – he's missing behind. I've seen him knock the tail feathers out of a pheasant. He's checking his swing as he pulls the trigger. He should be told to keep it going. The other one, the man in grey tweed, is shooting high. And the reason is that he's wearing a fishing hat with a low brim. He doesn't realize it, but when he tries to get his cheek down on the comb his hat-brim cuts off his vision so he lifts his head slightly. He should be told to take his hat off. Perhaps you could lend him a flat cap? I think those hints would come better from you than from me.'

'Good God!' said Mr Simon Watson MP. And again, 'Good God!'

The second drive went better. The sun was out but not blinding, there was just enough breeze to cool the brow and add interest to the marksmanship and the countryside was at its magnificent best. The Guns had got to know each other and had settled into the convention of leaving each bird to the Gun to whom it would pass nearest.

To solve the logistical problem, Ken met Joan before the third drive and handed over the Land Rover, going on in the beater's truck. Joan hurried home in the Land Rover, put the soup on to heat and the sausage rolls into the oven.

A pheasant drive may not take so very long, but directing everyone into place beforehand and later gathering up the bag and getting everyone moving again when they would rather stand around, drink in hand, discussing their successes and failures can be a lengthy procedure. Joan allowed herself plenty of time for loading the Land Rover. At what she guessed to be the appropriate moment she added the container of soup, the flasks of tea and coffee, the sandwiches and the box of sausage rolls and drove the length of a field to the Dutch barn where the beaters were to lunch.

She had guessed well. Minutes later the retired lorry that acted as transport for the beating team arrived at the barn. Ken had been swept off to assist with serving and entertaining the Guns at their more up-market lunch at the big house. Joan had been worried that very few of the beating and picking-up team would be known to her but even those who were strangers to her soon let their hair down. They proved to be a cheery and helpful group, about twenty in total, men drawn from all walks of life and age groups plus one sturdy woman with a son of about ten years old.

The barn was rather gloomy for such a cheery day and furnished only with a few wooden benches. Bemoaning the almost universal switch from the small straw bales that used to be so convenient as seating, the company soon had the trestle tables outside in the sunshine along with the wooden benches and set out where at least half the company could have the large, polythene-wrapped bales as soft and comfortable back-rests. They finished the unloading of their meal and the laird's beer on to the trestle tables and soon the whole company was seated, enjoying the rest, the sunshine and the food. Sam Smith, as driver of the game-cart, sat down with the rest.

Joan was aware of being regarded with curiosity. She considered retreating to the cottage and making another lunch for herself, but that might have led to her being considered 'toffee-nosed', which had always been one of her fears. So she took a seat in the middle of one of the benches and was introduced around.

Opposite her was a red-faced man with thinning red hair. He scrutinized her in silence for a minute and then said, 'So you're Kenny Whetstone's assistant. But you're not staying in the cottage he had when he was Jim McKee's under-keeper.'

'That wasn't considered suitable for a lone girl,' Joan said, 'especially with a rough lot like you around the place. I have a room in Ken's cottage.'

Nobody was quite brazen enough to enquire into their sleeping arrangements although Joan could feel questions hanging in the air.

One of the pickers-up, a vague-looking man in tartan tweed who had been handling the two most beautiful Labradors that Joan had ever seen, asked, 'Did Mrs Whetstone ever come back?' She was told later that he was one of the local vets, who did a little gundog training on the side.

'Not yet,' Joan said. It seemed to be a perfect chance to ask questions of a comprehensive cross-section of the rural population. 'I never met her, of course, but she does seem to have vanished rather suddenly – and mysteriously! What sort of person was she?' Perhaps, Joan thought, the use of the past tense might trigger something.

'A mantrap,' said a voice from further down the table.

'Mum, what's a mantrap?' asked the boy.

'I hope you don't find out the hard way.' The woman had an educated voice. Joan knew that she might be the wife of another beater or even of one of the Guns. Married women go beating for the sake of a day in the country, exercise, companionship and the customary bird or even a brace of birds to take home.

'Did she go off with somebody in particular,' Joan asked, 'or just go? Was anybody local not seen around for a while?'

There was a silence except for the sounds of a group of hungry men enjoying soup and hot sausage rolls.

'When was it, exactly?' asked a voice.

'Och, you remember,' said another voice unhelpfully. 'A little over a year ago.'

The red-faced man said, 'It was the day Kathie McKendrick died. They were talking about it at the funeral.'

Somebody at the other end of the tables started talking to his neighbour about Kathie McKendrick. Joan decided to intervene, as any startling revelations might be impeded by the presence of the boy. 'Charlie,' she said, 'we're running short of milk. Would you fetch a bottle from the fridge in the keeper's cottage? The door's not locked.' Obligingly, the boy got up and set off. 'Somebody met her cycling up the drive in mid-afternoon towards here,' Joan resumed. 'She gave him to understand that she was going home to pack her things – not that she seems to have taken much with her. She said that she was going away with another man. He thinks she was expecting to be picked up again shortly. If her lover was too shy to bring her all the way here, presumably he'd be too shy to come all the way to fetch her. Did anybody see her going back or meeting a lover?'

'Which drive was she using?' the lady asked curiously.

Joan had never thought to ask that

question but she had become familiar with the layout of the estate. A moment's thought brought the answer. 'It must have been the west drive, because they met and talked beside the water tower.'

'That would make sense,' said a stout man in corduroys. 'That's the one drive that isn't overlooked.'

'It's also the handiest to Newton Lauder,' said the lady.

Nobody seemed to have seen the lady on her return journey. 'I wonder what became of the bicycle,' Joan said. 'I can't see any new lover wanting to saddle himself with the lady's pushbike and scratch his car up in the process. Next shoot, I think we'll arrange it so that beaters go along both sides of the west drive.'

The boy was seen to be returning, bearing one bottle of milk, but the discussion would anyway have been ended by the cellphone that had been lent to Joan. It made a bizarre noise to attract attention and then informed her that the Guns would be moving off shortly.

When she was reunited with her employer's guests, Joan could hardly have missed the scent of good wines that hung around them. She made up her mind to have a serious word with Simon Watson, whatever the consequences to her employment prospects. Her own skin would be among those at risk and she was her daddy's girl.

Bearing that last fact in mind, she repeated the highlights her briefing speech before allowing shooting to resume. Perhaps it had some effect. Certainly, the rules of safety were obeyed even if marksmanship had suffered. During the last drive, however, a low bird came out of the sun and skimmed low towards the middle of the line. There came a single shot and several of the Guns ducked involuntarily.

Joan began to walk in the direction of Simon Watson, choosing words of reproof in her mind. *What a pity!* she thought. *It's been a good job while it lasted and we've almost finished the cottage…*

Simon Watson MP unloaded his gun and snapped it shut. 'I think I'll go and sit in the car,' he said loudly.

Twelve

To judge by the handshakes, the beaming faces and the scale of the tips, the day had proved a great success. The weather might have contributed to this, but a great deal of hard work had gone into preparations for the day, and the laird's guests, he had admitted to Joan, had been chosen for their compatibility rather than their skill with a shotgun.

A keeper's day is not finished when the last guest sets off for home, bearing with him a card proclaiming the day's bag and the names of the Guns in his pocket and the customary brace of pheasants in the boot of his car. (Technically, a brace comprises one cock and one hen, but with this shoot being concerned almost entirely with ex-laying hens that was not possible. A pair of hens is, presumably, just that – a pair.)

A good dinner, at home or in his host's house, may await the Gun, but for the keeper there remains work to be done. There is gear to be cleaned and put away and a last tour around to collect pegs, pick up dropped cartridge cases, close gates. Many of these chores could have been left until morning, at the risk of damage by farm animals, theft by locals and bad relations with farmers. Ken insisted on making sure that all was left in such a state that the farmer had little grounds for complaint to the landowner. On Joan's advice, however, they left one gate open where it could not possibly matter. A farmer with grounds for a good grumble is a happy farmer, but if he lacks something trivial to complain about he may happen on something more serious instead.

Ken and Joan, on that particular evening, had also received a message that Simon Watson wished to see them both next morning. There was a strong hint that his intention was to convey not only his own congratulations as a gratified host but also those of Lord Ellingham, who had been delighted to learn the explanation as to why his shooting had suddenly deteriorated since the purchase of a particular hat – so delighted, in fact, that he had gathered his fellow guests around him on the lawn and thrown the offending headgear high into the air, to be shot to shreds on his call. The tip that he had left with Joan had reflected his pleasure.

The night was late before the couple had managed to take a proper meal and tumble into bed. They were not given long to enjoy their well-earned rest. At about 3 a.m. Joan was roused by a hubbub of vehicles and voices.

'Something's happening,' she said into the pillow.

Ken had been on the go for almost twenty-four hours. 'It's not happening in here,' he said when she repeated the remark. He spoke without opening his eyes and fell immediately back into sleep.

Joan had been up and about for as long as her lover but she had not walked as many miles. Her plunge back into sleep was less precipitate. It soon dawned on her that, in addition to the various noises, a smell of smoke with a particularly unpleasant over-tone was percolating into the cottage and a red glow penetrated the thin curtains. She closed her eyes. A careful analysis associating the noises with the angle and brightness of the red glow as she remembered it was enough to assure her that whatever was burning was not threatening the cottage. Spontaneous combustion in a straw bale would be unusual but it was not unknown. Just why it should be accompanied by a smell of burning rubber was not worth staying awake to wonder. In seconds she was deeply asleep again.

Not even the self-important sounds of fire-appliance vehicles roused them. They woke at last to bright sunlight and the sound of hammering at the door. Joan slipped out of bed while Ken was still stretching and scratching. She had still not purchased any nightwear and was sleeping in one of Ken's shirts. Nobody was going to see her like that. She dressed hastily in yesterday's jeans and a clean blouse, kicked her feet into slippers and went to the door.

On the doorstep, dark in silhouette against a bright day outside, waited a woman in pearl-grey trousers with a matching jacket worn over a white top of stretch lace. The lady visitor's hair had seen the attention of a hairdresser within the last two days. Suddenly Joan was conscious of how far behind her she had left the world of hairdressers and smart clothes. Her hair, in particular, must look like a gorse bush.

It was not only the embarrassment of being caught *en déshabille* by one so immaculate that made Joan's spirits take a plunge. Her immediate reaction was that this was Ken's wife, come to take possession of her husband. This was followed by a realization that this lady did not correspond with any of the descriptions of Ken's wife that had been relayed to Joan, and she found it difficult to envisage why Mrs Whetstone would have come to reclaim her husband accompanied by a police constable in uniform.

The sudden appearance of the uniformed constable might have assured Joan that this was not her predecessor in Ken's bed, but it destroyed her peace of mind in another way. Joan, who had quite forgotten about any interruptions to her night's sleep, was immediately sure in her sleep-fuddled mind that her Edinburgh adventures had caught up with her. She was on the point of blurting out a denial that she had ever even heard of Craig and Grant the jewellers or gone by the name of Celia. Fortunately the constable spoke first. 'Is your husband in?' he asked.

'My partner's in. I think he's gone back to sleep. We're the two keepers and we had a very long day yesterday.'

'Oh.' This seemed to fluster the constable. 'I'm PC Brose, Lothian and Borders Police, and this is Detective Sergeant Lindsay. May we come in for a quick word?'

'What's it about?'

'Did the excitement in the night not wake you?'

Joan dredged back into a memory that was both clouded and sticky. 'I seem to recall hearing voices. And there was a red glow. But it was well away from here and my partner and I were both in a state of exhaustion.'

DS Lindsay stepped forward. 'We would still like a few words with both of you.'

'You couldn't come back a little later when we're both properly awake?'

'No, we couldn't.'

Joan forced a smile of sorts. 'Do please come in, both of you.'

She showed them into the sitting room and then escaped for a wash and a desperate attempt to tidy her hair. Before returning, she left Ken in the act of waking, with a cold, wet flannel in his hands.

'My partner will be ready in a few minutes,' she said, seating herself opposite the two police. 'Start with me if you wish.'

The constable produced the customary book and biro. The DS said, 'And you are?'

There would be no point in lying. 'Joan Lightfoot.' She waited for the axe to fall.

'And your partner?'

'Kenneth Whetstone.'

'Ah. And he is the man whose wife disappeared about a year ago?'

'I believe so,' Joan said. 'That was before I arrived here.'

'Which was when?'

'During the spring. I came here almost by chance and I started acting as Mr Whetstone's assistant immediately.'

The next question, logically, would have been to ask where she had come from. To Joan's relief, Ken, who seemed to have lingered only to use the cold flannel and to resume yesterday's clothes, made his appearance. He seated himself beside Joan and they linked hands. Joan thought what a scruffy – and therefore suspicious – pair they must look. Ken was overdue for a shave and although her own use of makeup was usually minimal she bitterly regretted the total lack of it.

'You are Mr Whetstone?' the DS enquired.

'Yes.'

'Do you know about the events of last night?'

'Only,' said Ken, 'that Joan nudged me and informed me that something was happening. I was exhausted, so I think I replied that it wasn't happening in here and I went back to sleep.' He yawned.

And there, Joan thought, went any chance that they might have had of persuading the police that they were partners only in the relationship of work. Detective Sergeant Lindsay seemed interested in pursuing this aspect. 'Tell me,' she said, 'are you two intending to get married some day?'

The question was double-barrelled and both barrels were loaded. Whatever Joan said would be wrong. While she hesitated, Ken, who had only awoken to half of the implications, spoke up like a gentleman. 'We intend to marry when we can,' he said.

'And when will that be?'

'You tell me,' Ken said gloomily.

'I think that you had better explain that remark,' the DS said.

Ken sighed and then spoke through clenched teeth. 'I mean that I had a wife who left me about a year ago. I don't know where she is or whether she's alive or dead. I don't particularly care, one way or the other, except that as soon as I can either divorce her or be sure that I'm free, we'll marry.'

'I see. Thank you. Did you know that the fire that caused the commotion in the small hours of this morning was caused by one of the straw bales from the row beside the Dutch barn? It had been dragged out into the field, stripped of the polythene wrapping, soaked in petrol and set on fire. In addition, some old tyres, scrap timber and fallen branches were heaped on top.'

'No,' Ken said. 'I didn't know that.'

DS Lindsay was looking ever more like a cat preparing to swallow some delicious and stolen morsel. 'And neither of you started the fire?'

'Certainly not,' Ken said. 'We were together all night.'

The DS said nothing at first but watched as the constable's pen recorded the answer. After the admission that they intended to marry, Joan thought, the police would not set much store by any alibi that they produced for each other. When Constable Brose had caught up, DS Lindsay said, 'Were you aware that a dead body was found in the ashes?'

There was a silence that lasted and lasted. Joan was aware of looseness in her bowels. Whether or not her life had been turned upside down might depend on the identity of the body. Then, as often, her mind sought escape in flippancy. Her first thought was to ask the sergeant whether, if the body should turn out to be that of Ken's wife, the officer would care to be a bridesmaid, but on further thought she realized that this would encompass all the thoughts that should never be allowed to surface. Before she could get around to formulating any more harmless comment, Ken had said, 'No, we bloody well were not. This is absolutely the first that we've heard about it.'

'Please allow your ... fiancée to speak for herself,' said the Detective Sergeant.

'I did not and do not know anything about a body,' Joan said.

'And you're not going to ask the identity of the corpse?'

'I was going to,' Joan said, loading her voice with patience. 'Then I realized that if it had been in a fire you probably hadn't had enough time to identify it. And, even if you knew its identity, you almost certainly wouldn't answer questions about it. You'll tell us when you're good and ready.'

The DS was nodding wisely. 'On the other hand,' she said, 'perhaps Mr Whetstone can help us. The body was female. That's all that we have been told for certain so far – that and the fact that the straw bale seems to have been one of last year's rather than this year's. Some preliminary questions suggest that the straw bale would have been made round about the time of Mrs Whetstone's disappearance. Obviously we have to consider the possibility that the body is hers. Can you tell us the name of her dentist?'

'She went to Mr Ogilvie,' Ken said. 'In Newton Lauder.'

'Did she have any distinguishing features?'

'Several minor birthmarks but nothing that would have survived a fire.'

'Do you have any photographs of her?'

Ken smiled without amusement. 'Not that I'm aware of. I certainly haven't treasured any romantic souvenirs. Any photographs that came my way usually got dropped into a shoebox in the bottom of the wardrobe, with a vague intention of sorting them all out in albums, probably as a harmless pastime for my old age. You might find her appearing in one of them. You're welcome to look.'

The sergeant did not immediately pursue the subject of photographs – which, Joan thought, suggested that the body was too badly burned for photographs to be of as much help as the dental records. Instead, 'Tell us about your relationship with your wife.'

'I think, Ken,' Joan said, 'that you ought to

speak to a solicitor before going into any detail.'

'My dear,' Ken said, 'I am not going to say anything that they could not find out by asking a few questions around the neighbourhood. Sergeant, I married at a time when I was employed by a university and doing some research into diseases of game birds. At first my wife appeared contented. She seemed determined to live up to what she considered to be my station in life. I, on the other hand, was totally uninterested in status and absorbed in my study area. Eventually, I became disenchanted with the academic life and wanted to get my hands dirty. I handed over my research and took the assistant keeper's job here. The drop in status – and money – brought about a change of attitudes. I was happier in my work than ever before but my wife became discontented. She had married me for the sake of status and long-term prospects and I had sacrificed them. Looking back, I can quite see that I was selfish.

'She became interested in other men and, frankly, I didn't care.' Ken was looking into the empty fireplace. He seemed to have forgotten that he had any audience. His appearance was seriously at odds with his educated voice. 'Whether she was looking for somebody who could keep her the way she wanted or whether she'd simply discovered that she liked sex after all I have no idea. I think, on the basis of no evidence, that she became promiscuous.

'That bothered me very little. I had stopped desiring her body and made it clear to her that I had no intention of acknowledging any child of hers as mine. To be fair to her, she still made my meals and did my laundry. And she continued to go out, cooking and cleaning for other households. The extra money helped a lot though I think the motivation was that she met single men that way. She didn't always come home at night, but she was quite honest about it. If she expected to be away for the night she'd tell me and leave everything ready for my breakfast. Really, she gave me very little cause for complaint. But she never told me who she would be with, and I wouldn't have expected it.'

The sergeant looked at him in exasperation. 'You surely must know the identity of at least one of your wife's lovers,' she stated flatly.

'I'm afraid not. I wouldn't let it worry you,' Ken said. 'I particularly wanted not to know.

The probability is that at least one or two of the men would be people that I met here or in the course of business, and I would have hated to be dealing with a syndicate member or a shopkeeper and have known that he was having sex with my wife. The more you try to banish that kind of thought, the more it keeps coming into your mind and it becomes very difficult to exclude it. But some of those identities must be common knowledge. Start asking around and you may find that everybody else is well aware of them. The husband is the last to know, so they say.'

'I suppose that's true,' the sergeant said. 'Isn't it, David?' There was some amusement in her tone.

The constable flushed. 'They say that he's the last to know that his wife's having affairs, not the identity of the lover.'

'I expect you'd know all about that.'

'May I ask a question?' said Joan.

The sergeant looked at her as though she had farted. 'You may ask it,' she said. 'I don't promise to answer.'

'I'm bound to find out eventually,' Joan said. 'It's this. Who's in charge of this case? It would surely be unheard of for a sergeant to remain in charge of a case involving a dead body and – surely? – foul play.'

It was the sergeant's turn to glow a dull red. It seemed that she did not enjoy being reminded of her lowly status. 'I suppose you're entitled to know,' she said at last. 'We're from Newton Lauder, where there's only a very small CID presence. Our boss, locally, is DI Fellowes. He's on holiday. I've spoken to him on the phone and he's coming back as soon as he can get a flight, whenever that may be. He's told me to do my best for the moment and try to gather as many facts as possible before witnesses forget, disperse or confuse each other by talking over the case. His superior in Edinburgh is Detective Superintendent Blackhouse, who has delegated oversight of the case to Honeypot.'

'Who?'

The sergeant's flush had been fading but now it returned at full strength. 'I'm sorry. I shouldn't have said that. Detective Inspector Laird. Laird is her married name. She was born Honoria Potterton-Phipps, and being somewhat attractive, wouldn't you say, David?' The constable nodded. 'The nickname Honeypot stuck. We may well see her through here if we don't make an early arrest,' the sergeant finished. 'I expect she's clearing her desk as we speak.'

Joan gathered that the presence of Honeypot would not be welcomed by the sergeant. Joan had been too startled by the arrival of the police and then by their news to consider their appearance except as compared to her own dishevelled state. Gradually she had absorbed the facts that the constable was thin and redheaded with protruding ears and that the sergeant, who was around thirty years old, had a round, pleasant face with good but undistinguished features. The sergeant's figure was a little on the plump side. Her recently tended hair was brown verging on fair. In short, Joan concluded, the sergeant was of the type that would pass for attractive among her male colleagues until a truly beautiful woman arrived for comparison.

DS Lindsay was not inclined to linger on the subject of Inspector Laird. 'Tell me about the day when your wife left you,' she said.

'One moment,' Ken said. He got up and left the room. Joan thought that he had probably heard a call of nature. The two representatives of the police may have thought that he was about to incriminate himself by resorting to flight, but he was back within a few seconds, carrying a file of papers. 'Mr Watson sent me on a two-day course at Marford Mill, about how a keeper should deal with poachers. And how he should liaise with the police,' Ken added without any great enthusiasm. 'These are my papers from the course and the notes I made at the time. You'll get the dates from them. When I got back here, there was no sign of my wife except that several people were eager to tell me that she had gone.'

'That's all very well,' said the sergeant. 'But can you prove that you attended the course? It would not be difficult to enrol for the course, not attend and fake the papers afterwards.'

Ken drew himself up in the chair. 'As it happens,' he said, 'I found myself at dinner with the Deputy Assistant Chief Constable, who was one of the speakers. At courses and conferences, you often get more out of the informal chats over the meal table than out of the formal sessions. I was surprised to find that he had a remarkably enlightened attitude to the problems of the keeper and he was also a shooting man and interested in the diseases of game birds. We got talking over a drink and it lasted until about three in the morning.

'Breakfast was at eight and it was followed

immediately by the first session. You'll see from the programme that it was a mock confrontation between a keeper and a poacher. I played the part of the poacher. I suggest that it would have taken an inspired driver in a supercar to get here from the Welsh border and back in the time, with enough margin in hand to commit a murder, bundle the corpse into enough straw to be picked up by the baler, start the machine up, wrap the whole bale and add it to the end of the row. What's more, the only vehicle I had the use of at the time was the old Land Rover outside the door. You're welcome to borrow it and try to do the double journey in that sort of time, even in the middle of the night.'

'I'll check the distances in the road atlas,' said the sergeant. 'I don't suppose any of the speed-camera films still exist, but there will certainly be a record if you were clocked speeding. Take the two together and we'll know if your alibi will stand up.' She switched her attention to Joan. 'Just for the record, where were you last year?'

If she had asked, *Where did you come here from?* Joan would have had a problem. As it was, she could answer honestly, 'This time last year, I was working for the Scillitoe agency in Edinburgh, temping, and staying in the YWCA. I didn't have a steady boyfriend and if I went out for a friendly drink it would be with another girl from the Y.'

The sergeant immediately lost interest in Joan. The latter could only hope that if her name were mentioned to Edinburgh City Police, nobody would make a connection with the Celia Lightfoot who was probably still high up on the wanted list. Ken was subjected to a half-hour of further questions, mostly covering ground that had already been raked over but extending to other employees on the estate.

At last the sergeant said, 'That will be all for now. Assuming that the body will prove to be that of Mrs Whetstone, this house is one of the places where she may well have been killed. It will have to be searched. There's a team on the way from Edinburgh. I'll have to ask you to leave the house to us for the rest of the day, but please stay nearby. There will be more questions.'

'We have our jobs to do,' Joan pointed out.

'This takes precedence. And today is Sunday.'

Joan was ready for her. 'You can tell them that the clothes in the spare room, which are in the wardrobe and all of the chest of drawers except the top drawer, all belong to Mrs

Whetstone. I haven't touched them. The law requires that we visit our traps every day. Are you ordering us to break the law?'

The sergeant closed her eyes for a long second – either in disgust, Joan thought, or to aid rapid cogitation. 'Of course not,' the sergeant said at last. 'You may go about your legitimate work but please be available again later today. And do not discuss the case with anyone.'

That, Joan felt, was going over the top. 'Have you been telling all the other locals not to discuss the case between them?' she asked.

The sergeant nodded.

'And what,' Joan asked, 'do you suppose they're all discussing at this very moment?'

The sergeant suddenly showed faint signs of being human after all. She even laughed. 'It's the usual form of words,' she said. 'When a case comes to court, it's sometimes necessary to be able to tell counsel that a witness was told not to discuss the case. It's purely rhetorical and nobody really expects it to have been taken seriously. And if anybody ever asks you in court, I did not say what I just said.'

'Of course not,' Joan said. 'We might be able to help you if you gave us an idea what you're looking for.'

The sergeant's moment of humanity had gone past. 'What do you mean?'

'I mean are you looking for a blunt instrument? A gun? Or a knife?'

The sergeant hesitated and then shrugged. 'We simply do not know and won't know until we have the results of the post-mortem. A straw fire with petrol as an oxidant, with rubber tyres added and the melting fat from a body can burn with a lot of heat and for a long time. For the moment, all we can do is to gather all the possibly relevant information and hope for the best.'

Ken had appeared inattentive. He suddenly said, 'May I ask to be informed as soon as you know the identity of the body?'

'Why do you ask?'

'Because I wish to know whether I'm free to have the banns read.'

Joan gave his hand a squeeze but the sergeant was thinking along less romantic lines. 'That wouldn't be in the belief that a wife can't be forced to give evidence against her husband? Because I rather think that a marriage contracted after the event would be discounted.'

Thirteen

Detective Sergeant Lindsay bustled self-importantly away, leaving PC Brose to accept the keys. The constable whiled away the time contentedly with an angling magazine that he found in the sitting room while Joan and Ken washed and tidied themselves and prepared for a day's work. Joan carried her shoes outside. When they were safely seated in the Land Rover, the constable locked up and strode off in the direction of the estate office, which, he explained, had been taken over as a temporary incident room. Estate business would for the moment be transacted from Mr Gracie's spare bedroom.

Ken reached for the ignition key. 'Better get on with it, I suppose.'

'Hold on,' Joan said. 'Curb your impetuosity.' It was an expression that an employer had once used to her and she had been waiting for a chance to make use of it. 'If they're going to make a search, they'll find that damned scooter and then the fat will be in the fire. We'd better get rid of it.'

Ken looked at her in dismay. 'You're right. But how the hell?'

'I am definitely not riding around on it,' Joan said. 'I can't afford to come to the attention of the fuzz. Let's get it into the back of the pickup. Then you can dump it somewhere while I visit the traps and top up the feeders and drinkers. Make the temporary home somewhere absolutely and totally cop-proof. My plan is that as soon as we possibly can, we drop it off on an Edinburgh street and phone the motorbike shop to say where it is. That way, everybody's happy and the matter dies the death. We can discuss the whole mystery later, but this seems urgent.'

Ken was silent until Joan thought that he was about to protest, but it seemed that he was only considering places. 'That sounds reasonable,' he said at last. 'I know just the place. I'll catch up with you somewhere around the pylon ride. If I can't see you I'll give a blast on the whistle and Dram should come to fetch me. Give me a hand. This is a time for togetherness if ever there was one.'

They had to turf the two dogs out of the open back of the pickup. 'Did you ever count yesterday's tips?' Joan asked as they wrestled with the heavy little machine.

'No. With a little luck the police will count them for us.'

'I just hope they're honest. Perhaps we'd better say that they've already been counted. Listen, I haven't had a new stitch to my back nor a pair of shoes for yonks. I hadn't really been bothered, living the life we do, until I saw the sergeant all smart and looking at me as though I was letting the side down.'

'You still looked far more desirable than she did.'

Joan was nearly distracted. 'You reckon? God bless you! They always say that love is blind. I rather think that she'd dolled herself up so as not to be put entirely to shame by this Honeypot person. Do you think we could afford some clothes for me now? Perhaps even for both of us?'

'I should think so. But don't bother about me. I still have some quite decent clothes in store, and I didn't want to ruin them living a keeper's life. Men's clothes don't date like a woman's.'

Together they heaved the scooter into the back of the Land Rover pickup and laid it on its side. Ken covered it with a square of sacking and drove cautiously away, avoiding the potholes. Joan set off on foot with the two dogs frisking happily round her. She put some thought into selecting the shortest possible route that took in all the traps and all the feeding areas. It was a good day for walking, as soon as the stiffness left over from the previous day had worn off. The topmost leaves of some of the tallest trees were turning brown and swallows were gathering on the overhead wires. She went first around the area that was least accessible by vehicle. Luckily it was their labour-saving habit to select one area of perhaps a quarter of the total shoot and trap it for a fortnight before moving all the traps to the next area. Ken caught up with her just as she finished topping up the feeders and drinkers in the area. He parked the Land Rover and joined her in visiting the traps.

'Done it,' he said. 'I got to know a chap who lives not far outside Newton Lauder and he gave me the use of a store behind his house. It used to be the gardener's toilet, but I'm not proud – it's dry and it's secure. I've been using it to keep my research records and my better clothes and property. My first cottage here was as damp as a puddle in winter and I'm not sure that this one's going to be much better unless we keep it warm.

There was nobody at home this morning so I just shoved the scooter in beside all my treasures.'

Whatever privations Joan might have suffered in her youth, cold and damp had never been among them. 'This cottage is going to be much better or I'll complain to our MP, who happens to be ... '

'Mr Watson,' they said together.

'Who does the store belong to?' she asked.

'A local shopkeeper and gunsmith. I've been buying all the shoot's cartridges and other supplies from him. Chap called Calder. Keith Calder.'

A happy chance encounter with Margaret Gracie and the mention of their exclusion from their cottage resulted in an invitation to a late lunch. The field between their cottage and the Dutch barn was partly enclosed by official-looking tape and busy with white-clad figures. They left the dogs in the Land Rover and sat down in her white-and-yellow kitchen to cold ham, hard-boiled egg and soft rolls.

'This,' Margaret said, 'is a bit of a carry-on.' She was wearing stretch jeans that exaggerated the size of her bottom and a stretch jersey top that did much the same for her pronounced bosom. Beside the lissom Joan, she looked definitely roly-poly but quite unconcerned about it.

'Isn't it just?' Joan said. 'But nobody tells us anything. You probably know more than we do. We slept in after yesterday's stresses and strains and we've been out around the shoot for most of the morning while all your neighbours were probably running to you with the tittle-tattle. Perhaps you can tell us what's been going on here.'

'I wish I could,' Margaret said. 'They've been running to me all right – they usually do – but mostly to ask me what's going on. Those who tried to offer me information obviously had the wrong end of at least one stick.'

'Oh dear!' Joan said mildly. 'You're usually the fount of all gossip. Well, we'd better pool what we do know. But first, let's clear the air.' She paused for some rapid thought. How could she express it so that her words when passed around, as they undoubtedly would be, helped to quell rather than rouse suspicions? 'There must be one topic in everybody's mind, and there's no point pussyfooting around it,' she said. 'I take it that everybody knows what was found?'

'The body? Yes, they do.'

'I was afraid so. They must be wondering – as we are, and so are the police – whether the ... what they found was the remains of Ken's wife. Obviously we're just as interested as anybody and more so than most because it does have a bearing on whether and when we can get married. But we know absolutely nothing.'

Margaret's eyes gleamed for a moment at the confirmation that Joan and Ken were contemplating matrimony. 'I can't help you much,' she said. 'I believe there's a team through from Edinburgh but none of the bosses has arrived yet, which gives Sergeant Lindsay a chance to strut her stuff. They keep asking people whether Mrs Whetstone had any distinguishing features and so far nobody's been able to think of anything much. They can't even agree how tall she was.'

Joan raised her eyebrows in surprise. 'They could get that from the clothes she left behind in the wardrobe.'

'I'll be damned.' It was Margaret's turn to show surprise. 'I'd always imagined her packing her bags neatly with lots of tissue paper and lifting them into her lover's car and the two of them driving off into the sunset. Which wouldn't have made much sense if that's her ... her. If it is and if she left her clothes behind, there couldn't have been much riding off into sunsets. She set a lot of store by those clothes. She was always a wee bit secretive about how she came by them, but she usually came running to me to show off any new acquisition.

'Anyway, I'll tell you what little I know. I think it was Harry – Harold, my husband – who saw the fire first from the bedroom window, but he decided that it was well away from everything and it was best left to burn itself out. He works hard, poor old boy, but he does need his sleep. From what they were saying – of course, you were right, there was a lot of gossip over the coffee cups – the first person conscientious enough to get out of bed was Sam Smith, but several other people arrived just after him. The general consensus seemed to be that there was no danger and that Harry's attitude had been the right one. Sam said that he wasn't sleepy anyway and he'd stay around and make sure that the stubble wasn't going to catch and no sparks were going to blow towards any buildings.

'Some timber had been added to the heap and a few old tyres and then petrol or diesel was poured over the lot. There's more burning than you'd think in a straw bale ... ' Her voice faded away.

'It's all right,' Ken said. 'You can say it aloud. There's a lot of burning in a body, especially when it's wrapped in straw. The fat melts and catches. And old tyres stoke up a fire like ... well, like blazes.' He attempted a laugh. He was trying to be very matter-of-fact but his hand was shaking.

Margaret nodded. 'Apparently it was several hours before it was cool enough to start raking over the ashes. One or two other people were with Sam when he started, and they saw something in the ashes that they took to be an animal or a child at first.'

'They lose a lot of bulk in a fire,' Ken said.

'So they're saying. Anyway, several different people called the fire brigade and the police and it all went from there.' Margaret got up from the table in order to fetch fruit, biscuits and cheese.

Ken took an apple and set about peeling it. 'You seem to have an efficient grapevine around here,' he said. 'The really critical thing is that, apart from me, the obvious suspects are my wife's former lovers.' He regarded his hostess anxiously. 'You did know ... ?'

'That she had lovers? Lord, yes! It's been a

matter of curiosity, and perhaps a little envy, among the ladies for a long time. Most women secretly desire a little polyandry.'

'Are you one of them?' Ken asked Joan.

'I'll leave you to worry about that.'

'The trouble,' Margaret said, 'was that, for obvious reasons, she rarely entertained her lovers at home. We'd see her ride off on her bike and somebody might see her waiting at the end of the drive to be collected, but whether by a lover or by somebody with some household jobs for her we'd no way of knowing.'

They fell silent while Margaret Gracie poured coffee. At last Ken said, 'Of course, any man collecting her by car could be fetching her to do a day's cleaning, while even a woman picking her up may unknowingly have been giving her a lift in the direction of an unfaithful husband. At the same time, Newton Lauder is well within cycling range. So I'm interested in knowing the identity of anyone who's been seen picking her up by car or who she's known to have worked for. Next time that the ladies foregather for coffee, would you at the very least listen? Perhaps even give the conversation a little nudge along the way?'

'Please do,' Joan said. 'I think you're the

only one of the ladies living around here – the wives of the estate staff – who we know well enough to ask for that sort of favour. And it does mean a lot to us.'

Margaret smiled graciously. 'I'm sure it does. I'll do what I can, short of accusing somebody Harry has to live and work with. But don't get fixated on the idea that everyone here is estate staff. Farms need a lot less labour than they used to, so now the surplus cottages are sold or let.' Margaret paused and looked plaintively from one to the other. 'What do we think actually happened?'

'I can only see one way of looking at it,' Ken said, 'and I'd expect the police to think the same way. Somebody wanted her dead. It could have been a sudden quarrel, a former lover who she was harassing or, of course, the police may suspect a betrayed husband.'

'A betrayed husband who has a shatterproof alibi,' said Joan stoutly.

'We knew that,' Margaret said. 'We've been telling each other that you were away on a course when she ran off or ... whatever she did do.'

'The person with a motive and an alibi is the first to be suspected,' Ken said. 'It was just after the harvest so the baler ... would have been standing out and probably still warm. As I remember it, the machine's a very quiet runner and when I came back from my course it was working near the Dutch barn. Once the bale was made up and wrapped, it could be added to the end of the row.'

'But why?' Margaret asked. 'I mean, why go to this rigmarole with a body that's going to be discovered anyway? Why not burn it straight away or else carry it off and lose it in – I don't know – water, or the foundations of a building or something?'

'I don't think it's as easy as that, to lose a body,' said Ken. 'People do disappear mysteriously and permanently but bodies often surface. And even if the guilty party has a car, everybody knows by now how the body's DNA can be detected in a vehicle. I can see the attraction of buying a year's delay while clues vanish, vehicles change hands and memories fade, followed by a fire just when that bale was next in line to be opened up and used as bedding or processed into cattle-feed.'

There was another thoughtful silence. Feet could be heard tramping up to the temporary estate office in the Gracies' spare bedroom.

'That suggests that we may possibly be looking for somebody who isn't here any more but went abroad,' Joan said. 'Somebody who was your wife's lover and who knows how to operate a baler.'

'I can't think of anybody who was here then and isn't here now,' Margaret said. She sighed. 'Leave it with me. I'll see what I can do. Don't expect miracles.'

'We won't,' Joan said lightly. 'We'll hope but not expect. Meanwhile, we have to face the sergeant. Worse, she seems to be in awe of the inspector who's probably coming, and from the way the sergeant spruced herself up I suspect that she – the inspector – may put us all in the shade. I don't know what one wears to be interrogated by a dishy inspector, though I still have an office frock that might pass muster. But my hair hasn't had more than a few passes with the magic hairbrush since I came here. Do you think all hell would break loose if I went into Newton Lauder this afternoon?'

Margaret shrugged and looked up at the ceiling. 'Probably. But in any case this is Sunday and even if they gave you an appointment there are only two hairdressers in the town and not a scrap of originality between them. You should really go into

Edinburgh tomorrow and spend real money. I'll tell you something. I may not be a genius with the scissors and comb but I'm better than either of those two locals. You really don't need more than a tidy-up. You have a natural wave that would take over if some of the weight came off. Would you like me to show you?'

Joan decided that her parting had been touched in so recently that it might not be noticed and that anyway she was not going to be seen by a senior and probably gorgeous police officer with her hair like a haystack. 'Go ahead,' she said. 'I'll be very grateful.'

'Not at all. Just don't tell everyone who did it or they'll all be wanting freebies. Come back in half an hour and I'll be ready for you.' Margaret got up but paused. 'And, by the way, Joan, you've been fishing the small loch, haven't you?'

'Now and again,' Joan said.

'Well, unless you've got written permission you'd better stop. I heard this morning that the owner of the cottage – with which the fishing on the loch is included – has come through for a visit. Apparently his cousin, who was going to buy the place, caught something nasty and died. So the owner, a

Mr O'Neill, came out from Edinburgh to make arrangements for selling the place. I understand that he'll be staying with Mr Watson.'

When they got outside, Joan joined Ken in the Land Rover, carefully closing doors and windows. 'Tasker O'Neill's coming to stay,' she said.

'Yes. You could treat yourself to a dose of summer flu, or even go to visit a sick grandmother. On the other hand, if you find that you can't avoid him you should have a quick and private word with him and explain that if he drops you in the muck you'll tell the world about his generous treatment of you.'

'I hear that my granny is coming out in spots,' Joan said glumly. From the open back of the Land Rover, Dram looked at her hopefully. 'You stay where you are,' Joan told her.

'This isn't your natural colour,' Margaret said. They were back in the yellow and white kitchen and Joan had a tablecloth round her neck.

'No.' Joan always felt impelled to shake her head while giving a negative answer, but head-shaking was not to be recommended while sharp scissors were being plied round about. She kept her head still. 'I just like myself better this way.'

'There's no answer to that.' Margaret would have said more but they were interrupted by a knock on the door and the entrance of the young girl who acted as general dogsbody in the farm-and-estate office. 'Mr Watson was on the phone,' she said. She spoke with reverence. Apparently there were still some of the up-and-coming generation who were prepared to be impressed by a Member of Parliament or a landowner – or, at a pinch, both. 'He wanted to find Miss Lightfoot. He wants you to come up to the house.'

It seemed that Mrs Gracie was not so easily impressed. 'Call him back. Tell him that we'll be another half-hour here. Damn!' she said as the door closed. 'Now it will be all over the district that I give free haircuts.'

Joan moved very slowly to catch herself in the mirror. 'But will it be all over the district that you give *good* free haircuts?' she asked.

Margaret chuckled. 'Judge for yourself in a minute.'

'I could always grumble to anyone who'll listen that you charged me the earth.'

'Now you're talking.' Margaret was silent for a minute while she tidied around Joan's left ear. 'I bumped into old Gerry this morning. He was talking to a couple of the ladies. He seemed to be hinting that he knew something that nobody else knows. He's a malicious old beggar and you can't always believe a word he's saying but it might be worth your while sounding him out. I can't do it. He's hated my guts ever since I ticked him off for spreading gossip about Simon Watson and his housekeeper.'

'Was there any truth in what he was spreading?'

'I would be amazed.'

Fourteen

It seemed unlikely that Mr Watson would have issued such a peremptory summons, and only to Joan, in order to offer his congratulations on a successful day. She could easily think of a dozen things that she would rather be doing than discussing with the laird her position and Ken's with regard to the events of the night and those still unfolding. There were so many unknowns that she might well feel that she was fending off a swarm of bees with a walking stick. However, when the landlord and employer calls, you go – unless, of course, you are Mr Lightfoot Senior, in which case you defy him and get the sack instead.

Joan duly presented herself at the house. This was a substantial building in Victorian baronial, but the grim frivolity of the style was softened by the later addition of sundry porches, conservatories and greenhouses. She was admitted by the housekeeper. For much of each year, Mr Watson was absent at Westminster and only at home for hurried weekends during which his attention was focused more on constituency business, clinics and public meetings than on personal comfort or entertaining. Thriftily, he kept only that lady as permanent staff, any shortages while he was at home being made up by part-time help from local ladies as and when required. The widowed housekeeper, a Mrs Charles, was a petite lady but a ball of energy. She had a round face with a small, hooked nose and a pursed mouth – a not unattractive combination but hardly alluring enough to invite the attention of even such a gossipmonger as old Gerry.

Mr Watson was at work. His study, on the

first floor of the big house, was appropriately large and his two desks, one for estate business and one for parliamentary issues, were in proportion. The room itself was decorated tastefully but severely as befitted its function, but superficially disordered by an ebb and flow of paper. Joan judged that he was a naturally tidy person but that this tendency was defeated by his refusal to delegate or to cull and by the sheer volume of material, much of it arriving in the form of emails and faxes so that while they spoke the printer on an adjacent table was regularly adding to the accumulation of paper in the basket. Rumour had it that his hardworking part-time secretary had been promised a spell in the dungeons of Westminster if she tidied any papers without his express direction.

He looked up as Joan was shown in and then, taking in Joan's improved appearance, after glancing at her jeans to be sure that she was not importing too much mud or chaff, half rose while he indicated the chair opposite. Joan gave full marks to Margaret for her styling. The old, unkempt Joan would not have merited such courtesy.

'First,' Mr Watson said stiffly, 'I owe you my congratulations on the running of yesterday's shoot. McKee might have produced more birds, though even that is open to doubt, but he could never have presented them as well or made the day run as smoothly.' At this point he showed signs of a very appropriate embarrassment. 'And, perhaps, I also owe you an apology. We all know the subject and it won't happen again. Please convey the congratulations also to Ken Whetstone. Am I forgiven?' Joan inclined her head graciously. He hastened on to a pleasanter subject. 'We have a syndicate shoot booked for a week next Saturday. Do we have enough birds left on the ground?'

Joan had looked around with that very calculation in mind. 'I think so. The new birds round the Knoll are growing on well. If the syndicate hasn't fired enough shots by mid-afternoon – whether they hit anything is their problem – we could fit in one extra drive there.'

The laird smiled but shook his head. 'Not with a let day coming up after another ten days. We'll just have to plan the syndicate shoot for maximum difficulty. High, fast birds coming out of the sun.' The serious matters disposed of, he moved on. 'This other thing is a less happy business. Presumably the body is or was Mrs Whetstone. How is Ken taking it?'

'He's taking it well,' Joan said. 'He and his wife seem to have been estranged for some time before she disappeared, so he's no more emotionally involved than anyone else ... except for the possibility that he may now find himself free to marry again. I hope that you haven't forgotten sending him to attend a course that same weekend and then meeting her and being told that she was running away?'

'I do remember all that,' he said seriously. 'I shan't forget.' He leaned back in his chair and put the tips of his fingers together. 'I just ask one favour from you. Assuming that the body does turn out to have been Ken's wife, you'd be less than human if you didn't listen and ask questions. You have a lot at stake and yet no direct personal involvement. People may talk to you. What I'm asking is that you give me early warning if you see any signs of a scandal that might hurt me or anybody on the estate. No need to look surprised. Those who live here are mostly my tenants and all of them are my constituents. I try always to do my best for them.'

Joan was aware that an appearance of sincerity was any politician's first stock-in-trade, but his manner certainly carried conviction. Her opinion of the MP had diminished when she had seen him lapse and take a dangerous shot. Now it began to recover. 'I think that's very commendable,' she said.

He smiled faintly, nodded acknowledgement and made no further comment. 'I have one more favour to ask,' he said. 'I have a guest here, a Mr O'Neill. He owns that cottage down by the loch. The fishing rights to the loch are included with it, but I hope to buy them back from him. He's come to arrange for the disposal of the cottage and the estate will probably make an offer, but there's no need to tell him that. He seems to have lost his own keys to the place, but I have the emergency set here.' He reached out to hand her a ring of keys. Joan was wearing a fleece that properly belonged in the cottage by the loch. An identical ring of keys was still in the pocket. 'I'd be grateful if you'd take the Range Rover and convey him round there. He wants to remove any personal possessions before putting the place into an agent's hands. I'd take him there myself except that I'm expecting an important phone call.'

The mild pleasure of discussing the shooting programme gave way instantly to a hollow feeling of doom. Distracted by her efforts to conjure up a satisfactory excuse, Joan nearly said that there were very few personal possessions there other than the indecorous magazines, but she remembered in time that she was not supposed to have been in the cottage. Could she simulate a convincing appendicitis? A stroke? Perhaps a moribund grandmother would do the trick. But before she could complete her list, let alone make a selection, Mr Watson said, 'Ah, here he is now,' and Tasker O'Neill walked into the room.

The laird performed a brief introduction and then turned away to answer the telephone, leaving no doubt that this was the important call that he had awaited. Meanwhile, Joan was rather hoping for a thunderbolt. Tasker O'Neill began by accepting the introduction at face value but then his polite and slightly condescending glance sharpened. Joan could see recognition dawning. He opened his mouth, whether to greet or denounce her she had no time to guess. Mr Watson was already on the phone and scrabbling one-handed among his papers.

Tasker smiled suddenly and gestured to Joan to precede him out of the room. Dumbly, she led the way down to where the Range Rover waited on the gravel forecourt and got into the driver's seat. A very new Jaguar was parked crookedly beside Mrs Charles's old Mini, so Tasker had changed his car for a newer model. He seemed to be in no hurry to speak.

'You wish to visit the cottage by the loch?' she prompted him.

'Yes indeed.' He studied her for a few seconds. 'That hair colour suits you. Of course, it isn't your natural colour. I should know.'

Joan refused to be thrown by reminders that he had seen her hair when it remained its natural colour. She started the car. The radio came on. She let it play. He reached out and turned down the volume. 'So this is where you've been hiding out, Celia.'

'Please don't call me that,' she said. 'I've gone back to my real name. Joan.'

'Much more suitable. Tell me, Joan, have you granted an interview to the Edinburgh police?'

'Do you think I'd still be walking around here if I had?'

'That's what I wanted to know,' he said obscurely. He seemed pleased about something. 'How did you come to meet the new man in your life so quickly?'

She was turning out of the drive on to the

road. When the manoeuvre was complete she said, 'None of your damn business.'

'There's no need to be like that.' She could hear amusement in his voice and feel the vibration of a chuckle. 'I've got you where I want you, so be polite. Where did you stay, in between leaving my flat and moving in with your gamekeeper?'

'Same answer.'

'Not very nice. When I think of what we've been to each other ... ' Glancing sideways at his podgy form and broken veins, thinking about what they had once been to each other and seeing Ken's fit body in her mind's eye made Joan feel slightly sick. 'Do you think the police would like to know where you are now?' he asked.

'Do you think the world would like to know how you treated me?' she retorted.

'I dare say that I'd live it down quicker than you would.'

Thoughts bumped and jangled in Joan's mind. As she turned off on to the track to the loch she said, 'You still owe me over a hundred quid in wages.'

He seemed to be too busy to answer, holding on by the grab-handles as she nursed the Range Rover over the humped and potholed track. Beyond the forestry, the view over the loch and the cottage came into sight. The more open ground was dotted with well-grown pheasants sunning themselves, but with the approach of the vehicle first one, then several and finally all the flock flushed and headed home to the release pen. The scene had somehow become less friendly than before. The presence of its far from loveable owner seemed to taint it. The edge of a cloud came over the sun and she felt a shiver.

She pulled up in front of the cottage, jumped out quickly and, while unlocking the door, managed to palm the original set of keys. She had wondered, earlier, why anybody should have gone to the trouble and expense of including a post box in the door but now she knew that it had been for her sole benefit. Hiding the act with her body while Tasker was still climbing stiffly out of the Range Rover, she posted the original keys through the letter box. When he arrived, she handed him the other ring of keys. 'All yours,' she said. 'I'll wait in the car.'

He shook his head violently. 'No you don't. I want you inside. Come on.' As he pushed into the cottage his foot moved the keys on the mat. He looked down at the sound, then looked at the other keys in his hand. 'Hullo! These must be the keys I've been looking for.'

'At a guess, you dropped them outside, last time you were here, and somebody picked them up and popped them through the slot.'

'No. I was hunting for them at home. I knew where I'd put them and they'd gone.' The penny dropped suddenly and he grinned as wolfishly as a stout and dissipated man could possibly manage. 'Now I understand. You were living here as my guest. That's how you met your gamekeeper. The hundred pounds you say I owe you wouldn't cover a week's rent.'

What he said was perfectly true, so Joan preserved a dignified silence. Tasker started to sort out the contents of the cottage. Into an untidy heap in the middle of the floor went most of the clothes from the cupboards and the air rifle from the gun safe. 'I must admit that you left the place neat and clean,' he said. He tested the gun safe but it was well secured and obviously heavy. 'You're taller than I am.' He indicated the fishing rod and she lifted it down for him. 'Plastic,' he said disgustedly. The rod was carbon-fibre and very expensive, but he had never been a devotee of field sports. He added it to the heap along with the fishing bag.

In a common carrier bag he had collected some of the ornaments, two clocks, an electric knife and a set of spoons. Another carrier bag was carefully closed but she guessed that it held the smutty magazines. This, apparently, was all that he intended to keep. He indicated the pile in the middle of the floor. 'Even if they were my style, those clothes wouldn't fit me. You can have all these things.'

'I can?'

'I am not going to wear second-hand clothes. Your need is greater than mine. From the look of you, you can't afford to be too fussy. Dump it all outside and you can come back for it. It should be worth more than your hundred pounds, but I can't see myself haggling with a dealer over it. What would you do about the furniture?'

The air rifle and the trout rod alone were worth several hundred. The keeper's cottage now had the suite from the big house but the rest of the furniture was frankly rubbish. 'I'll give you another hundred for it,' she said.

'Where would you get a hundred pounds?'

'Out of yesterday's tips.'

He raised his eyebrows. He had never been a generous tipper. 'All right. You have a deal.'

'And you won't tell the police where I am?'

He smiled again. She preferred him when he didn't smile. 'No, I won't tell the police where you are. You can trust me on that.' He slipped the door key off the ring. 'Post it though the letter box again when you've finished.' She put out her hand. He closed his fist. 'When I've got my hundred,' he said.

'All right. But if you try slipping me the wrong key I'll take a chainsaw to the door.'

'You're very suspicious.'

'You've given me grounds.'

He took hold of her wrist. 'That isn't all that I've given you. I've been very generous. Now might be a good time to start repaying me.' He put an arm round her and groped for her breast, at the same time pulling her towards the bedroom.

Joan found herself torn. He was not asking her to do anything that she had not done a dozen times before – or, at least, so she believed. She could lie back and plan the drives for the syndicate day. But the loving of Ken had changed her. She awarded Ken full marks as a lover. When he embraced her it was truly an act of love and not a mere quenching of his own desires. To accept one of Tasker's tawdry salutes would sully all of Ken's.

'Bugger off,' she said.
'You weren't always so fastidious.'
'But since then, I've known the loving of a real man.'
His frown reminded her of the storm clouds that had preceded her first encounter with Ken. 'I can still tell the police where you are,' he said.
'If you wish. I think I would prefer that.'
To her surprise, he laughed and let go of her wrist.

She drove straight to the keeper's cottage and unearthed the remains of her ill-gotten hoard from a tea caddy in the darkest corner of the kitchen's darkest cupboard. The thickness of the wad seemed to be about right, but the contents of the cupboards seemed to have been disturbed so she could only assume that the police were honest. She took out a hundred and gave it to him when they stopped outside the front door of the big house. At their parting, they exchanged the fewest possible words. Joan walked back to the keeper's cottage. The Land Rover was back outside the door with Ken pottering helplessly in the kitchen. Since Joan's arrival he seemed to have forgotten how to feed himself.

'I haven't had any tea,' Ken said plaintively.

Joan patted his hand. 'Nor have I. Quick tea coming up and then I need you and the Land Rover for what's left of the daylight.'

They ate toasted cheese and bacon in haste while she explained the deal she had made. When, an hour later, they stood in the cottage, Ken looked around with his eyes wide open. 'You bought this lot for a hundred quid?'

'Plus a hundred or so that he owed me for secretarial services and which I wasn't going to get anyway. He was saving himself the bother of arguing with dealers.'

'All the same, the air rifle and the fishing gear alone must have cost a thousand.'

'But he didn't know that,' Joan said happily. 'A clear case of *caveat vendor*. If the bonfire's still smouldering, I suppose they wouldn't let us put our old furniture on it?'

'Not a chance,' said Ken. 'We'll have a bonfire of our own. Do those clothes fit you?'

'You've seen me in some of them,' Joan said. 'They're men's clothes but perfectly suitable for a lady keeper on a shooting day. Tweed breeks, green wellies and a flat cap. What could be better?'

'You'll have to be careful. If you turn out better dressed than the guests, they may decide that we don't need the tips.'

'Barbour coats and green wellies are universal,' she pointed out.

The furniture was bulkier than she had thought. Dram had to travel at Joan's feet. When they were on the way back along the drive with the first load, Joan said, 'One thing bothers me. Tasker O'Neill inherited the cottage before I met him. He must have visited here from time to time. Did he ever fish?'

'He did come here regularly for a few months while he was making his mind up whether to keep the place or not. He tried fly-fishing once or twice. I tried to teach him to cast but he never did get the timing right. No hand-eye coordination. Why?'

Dram was trying to climb into Joan's lap but was pushed firmly down. 'Because when I wanted to change flies I looked for a pin to clear the eye of one fly with. I found a brooch in the bag – quite a sensible tool for the job, because you can clip it shut and not be in any danger of jabbing the pin into yourself. And Tasker's a wealthy man with an eye for a woman and not much else. Just the type your wife might have made a beeline for. And I could imagine him getting quite ruthless and vicious with a woman who tried to put pressure on him. He's changed his car recently, which might suggest that he was getting rid of any contact traces.'

'Very interesting,' Ken said. He pulled up in front of his cottage. 'Let's have a look at the brooch.' Joan opened the bag and picked carefully through fly boxes, small tools, a priest and several reels of nylon. At last she came up with a gold brooch. Evidently there had been a stone that was now missing. 'I couldn't be sure,' Ken said. 'If I knew what colour of stone belonged in it my memory might be jogged. Perhaps the forensic scientists could find a trace of it. This could take the heat off me.'

'And transfer it to me,' Joan said. 'Use that academic brain of yours for a minute. How long would it take the police to make the connection?'

'It's a tenuous sort of link. I don't think they'd make the connection at all.'

'*Don't think* isn't quite good enough. They wouldn't even have to make the connection for themselves. As soon as Tasker found himself being interrogated he'd be sure that I'd shopped him and he'd be falling over himself to drag me into the shit with him. If the police find that brooch for themselves, well and good. But don't go pointing it out to them.'

Fifteen

They had almost finished unloading the first shipment when a smart Range Rover, almost a clone of Mr Watson's vehicle, arrived and parked nearby, making the Land Rover look very tatty and exhausted. At a second look, Joan recognized that this Range Rover, in addition to being top of the range, differed from Mr Watson's vehicle in having been given the full upgrading by Messrs Overfinch, a treatment which would have added many thousands to its already substantial cost.

Detective Sergeant Lindsay emerged, followed by a very elegant lady. Detective Inspector Laird was dressed modestly yet the woman's eye recognized that she was in the height of fashion. Since leaving the care of Tasker O'Neill, Joan had had little personal contact with the world of couture, but she had contrived to buy, beg or borrow copies of ladies' magazines from her new neighbours. She decided that there must be more money around than even two police salaries could provide. (Later, she was told that Honeypot's father was an industrialist and a major landowner.)

The inspector, she noticed, had perfect features illuminated by a look combining humour with sexuality. And as though this were not enough to make any other woman grind her teeth, she seemed quite unaware that her appearance would cause any normal male to slaver. Joan was glad that her own hair was freshly dressed and that her obvious engagement in physical tasks was sufficient excuse for her attire.

The sergeant seemed to feel that the usual cursory mentioning of names and ranks was not sufficient. She carried out introductions as though presenting a scullion to royalty. The inspector, however, was less concerned with rank and shook hands with each of them.

'Do you wish to see us both together?' Joan asked. 'Because, if not, I could go and finish what we were doing. The owner wants a cottage cleared for sale and I bought the loose furniture off him to replace the rubbish that came with this cottage. There's not much still to move, and none of it heavy.'

'I would prefer that,' said the inspector, smiling. She stooped to fondle Dram's ears. 'Strange as it may seem, people sometimes feel that they can speak more freely to me without their partners being present.'

Joan wanted to ask whether that applied to men rather than women. Instead, she climbed into the Land Rover and drove away, trying to avoid the potholes in case a loud rattle should betray its humble state. Dram had decided that the two officers were trustworthy and opted to stay with Ken. Tanya had begun spending her daytimes with Mr Watson, her true owner.

At Loch Cottage, it took only minutes to load the Land Rover with the remaining two chairs and a mirror, with cushions and clothing packed between and around. The fishing bag had gone with the first load but the rod was still in the cottage and there were two perfectly suitable flies on the cast. If she dallied for quite a lot of time, Inspector 'Honeypot' Laird might well decide that Joan's evidence, in view of her late arrival in the area, would not be worth waiting for.

The day was warm but the sun was now obscured and there were flies dancing above the water, perfect for fishing. She took the rod down to the water's edge and began casting.

She landed one trout of about a pound and a half almost immediately but then the action seemed to cease. However, she had proved to herself that she was suitably equipped and that the fish were taking, so she fished on without so much as a nibble for another hour, moving along the bank and back again.

There were patches of weed in the loch where the insects were hatching, but she knew the position of each patch, so it was a surprise when her line suddenly checked. Instead of vibrating with the struggles of a fish it remained taut and sullen. She tried varying the direction of her pull, but although something on the end of the line could be moved slightly it was a limited pull and a sluggish movement. Whatever had snagged her line was about ten yards from the bank and in waist-deep water.

Without a reserve of leader and flies, her fishing was over unless she could free her line. Nylon or polycarbonate leader, she knew, provided that knots had been tied with due care, can often take substantially more tension that its nominal rating. She gave a pull and steadily increased its strength. Just before the line snapped, something showed above the surface. The exposure was too short for her to focus on it, but retained in her memory was an image of a shape and texture resembling a segment of a bicycle tyre. Then the leader parted and her line flicked back over her shoulder.

If her fleeting impression was not deluding her, this could be very significant. She had fished this stretch of water often and had never been snagged before. There had not been a sudden spate to bring down a tree branch. To call this to the attention of the police when it might be something irrelevant would entail explanations that she did not want to make. She tried to visualize quite innocent objects that would accord with her remaining impression but could only imagine the trunk of a very small elephant, which seemed even less likely than a bicycle. Her mind, she knew, was finding refuge in irrelevancies and away from thoughts of murder.

She decided to look for herself. If there should happen to be a bicycle, and a lady's bicycle at that, it would be time enough to invoke the authorities.

A careful look and listen suggested that she had the place to herself. She even walked to where the path from the farm buildings emerged suddenly from behind a clump of rhododendrons. Feeling safe, she removed everything below her waist and tucked her blouse up into her bra. A conveniently shaped stick lay on the bank. She collected it and lowered herself into the water. This was cool but not too cold. The mud worked squishily between her toes and threatened to let her slide and fall. A wading staff would have been a mighty help but she made do with her stick.

The water was lapping near her navel when her foot struck something that was neither mud, stick, stone nor waterweed. She balanced herself carefully and probed with the stick, which had a conveniently broken-off twig at the base. A little probing and a good twist and the stick seemed to have found a grip on something. She pulled, lost the grip and found it again and raised what was definitely a bicycle's front wheel to the surface. The mud did not have a firm grip, so the machine had not been there for long.

She turned, intending to tow the bicycle to the shore. Out from behind the screen of rhododendrons plodded the elderly figure of Gerry the farm worker. Over his shoulder was a large scythe, lending him a resemblance to Old Father Time. Even in that fraught moment she realized that bringing a tractor towing a mower into that secluded area would present problems of access. Doubtless Gerry had been given the task of keeping grass and weeds down around the cottage. And Gerry was just the sort of person who would inevitably turn up at the worst possible moment.

Stark naked as she was from the soles of the feet to just below her bosom, she had no intention of emerging from the water while he was there. This was partly due to the ingrained female instinct not to attract unwanted male attention but also because of the tales he would no doubt spread around the locality. She let the bicycle sink again. While she hesitated, he walked straight towards her and stirred her neat pile of clothes with his toe.

'What you doing in there?'

'I was fishing and my line snagged on something. Kindly mind your own business and go away.'

He stooped, picked up her panties and held them up to the light. 'Very pretty. Hey, you're bare-arsed?'

'Never you mind. Just go away.' She worded it rather more strongly than that.

'I got my job to do.' He grinned, showing gaps among his surprisingly white teeth, and dropped the underwear back on the other clothes. He made a pass with the scythe. 'Takes me a good hour, usually. Sometimes longer. Depends on things like the weather. You think it's going to hold?'

Despite the cooling effect of the water, Joan could feel her blood pressure building. She was sure that small creatures were wriggling between her thighs. The mud was threatening to let her feet slide so that she would sit down, probably on the bicycle. Tears were not far off but she was damned if she was going to let him see them. 'Get out of here, you old horror,' she said – she could hear her voice going up the scale – 'or I'll ... I'll ... '

'You'll what?' He flourished the scythe. It looked very sharp. 'There's a thing called self-defence.' Joan stood and endured a lecture on the legal concept of self-defence. Gerry's ideas about the law on that subject were exaggerated and quite a long way from being accurate, but that only made him the more dangerous. She seethed.

She still refused to come out of the concealment of the water, but she could at least assume the offensive. Her toes found a stone. She kicked it towards the bank where the water was shallower. When her modesty was only just preserved she accepted getting a wet shoulder and sleeve, plunging down to grab up the convenient missile. This turned out to be a smooth stone about the size of an apple. In her youth, she had been conscripted into many games of cricket with her brothers and she could throw straight. He disbelieved either her intention or her skill because he was too late to duck. Her throw caught him on the side of his jaw.

'So that's the game we're playing?' He hunted in the grass for where the stone had fallen. When he found it, he threw it back with force and accuracy. She was just in time to duck. The stone splashed into the water somewhere in the middle of the loch. He searched for another. She retreated.

Her toes found no more useful stones but instead made painful contact with the bicycle. This was too big to throw but might form some sort of shield. She dragged it up. The front wheel with its dozens of spokes did indeed form a shield. Gerry straightened up with several stones clutched between his body and his left arm. Between the spokes, she saw his next throw coming straight for her eyes, but it bounced back.

'Is this what happened to Mrs Whetstone?' she asked.

He checked in the act of winding up for another throw. 'What's that supposed to mean?'

She pointed a finger at him. 'You did it. You made a pass at her. Or she caught you being a Peeping Tom. She was going to report you so you hit her with a stone and you hid her body in a straw bale. When you heard that I was going to start the next shoot with a beat along the sides of the drive, you recovered the bicycle and dumped it in the loch.'

For a full minute he considered that scenario. Then he said, 'Balls!' and threw his stone. She was just in time to get down behind the shelter of the bicycle wheel.

For how long could this go on? Quite a long time, she decided. But how long before a stone found a space between the spokes large enough let it through? The sensible answer would be to sit down in the water, covering her face with the hub of the wheel and the spokes where they were closest together. After all, she was already about as wet as she could possibly get. She was about to let herself subside when rescue arrived unexpectedly. There came the crisp mutter of a well-tuned engine and the inspector's Range Rover was descending the track from the gap in the plantation.

Gerry dropped his stones. Joan dropped the bicycle and began waving.

The Range Rover stopped just a few yards away. The inspector got out, followed by Ken. Ken was followed by quite the most beautiful black Labrador that Joan had ever seen, more beautiful even than the pair that the vet had been working on the shoot.

First things first, Joan decided. 'I've got something here that will interest you,' she said.

Gerry, it seemed, had not vented all his spite. He still had some to spare. His ugly old face broke into a grin. 'You've got something there that will interest us all,' he cackled.

That did it. Joan made for the bank, intending, bare-arsed or not, to leap out and claw his face off. Later she was sure she could remember the feeling of steam coming out of her ears as in a cartoon. But Ken had already assessed the situation and studied the clothes on the bank. He rescued the trout rod from its position almost under the wheels of the vehicle and, placing the top ring between her breasts, pushed. The rod bent into a hoop but his action was enough to bring Joan to her senses. She reversed until she could feel the bicycle against her ankle. 'This,' she said, stooping to pull it up into view. 'Ken can tell us if it's his wife's bike.'

'Put it on the bank,' said the inspector, 'and then come out of there.'

'I'm not coming out until that old voyeur has gone, preferably into custody,' Joan said. 'I don't have a stitch on below my waist. He refused to go away and he threw stones at me.' Ken looked like thunder and moved closer to Gerry. The Labrador took a seat near Joan's clothes and became an interested observer.

The inspector glanced quickly from Joan to Gerry and then to the clothes on the bank. 'I see,' she said. 'Then we'll deal with this little matter first. What goes on?'

'I was clearing out the last things from the cottage. The trout rod was one of them. I thought I'd give you a little extra uninterrupted time so I decided to try a few casts.'

'Any luck?' the inspector asked. She sounded interested but Joan wondered whether this was not just a check on her story. Joan had put her first fish on the damp grass under a large dock leaf. She pointed to it. The inspector and her dog made suitably admiring noises.

'Much later,' Joan said, 'I got caught up in what turned out to be the bicycle. The fishing bag with the rest of the flies had already gone to ... our home, so I stripped off and waded in to try to rescue the broken cast. I found the bicycle, but that old Peeping Tom arrived and wouldn't go away.'

'When I arrived,' said the inspector to Gerry in awful tones, 'you were throwing stones at the young lady.'

'She started it,' Gerry protested.

'All that I saw,' said the inspector, 'was you throwing stones at her.' She paused and looked at Joan. Some kind of intuitive signal passed. 'If she cares to press a charge ... '

'I hear,' Joan told Gerry, 'that you've been boasting that you have some information that the rest of us don't know about. It was most likely about some lover of Mrs Whetstone's. I can't think what else it might be.'

Gerry uttered a monosyllabic word of denial.

'Has the body been identified as hers?' Joan asked.

The inspector gave an involuntary nod. 'You didn't get it from me,' she said, 'but it'll be all over the place by tonight. Yes. The dental evidence seems conclusive.'

'Then go ahead and charge him,' Joan said. 'He arrived while I was in the water investigating the bicycle. He saw from my clothes that I was bare ... bare from the waist down and he refused to go away. And when I wouldn't come out he threw stones at me.' This would have been a good time to let the tears come, but unfortunately they seemed to have deserted her. 'I'm beginning to freeze,' she said. 'Can't you take him away? I'll press charges. Unless he talks damn quick.'

The inspector made a face. It seemed that she was ignoring all proper rules and procedures, but information was information. 'Well?' she said.

'It was nothing,' Gerry said. 'Nothing at all.'

'Then you may as well tell us. Unless you want to find yourself in court.' Honeypot hid a smile. 'That sort of conduct is covered by an act dating from the time of James. The penalties may be considered excessive ... '

'All right,' Gerry said. 'All bloody *right*! I'll tell you. It was young Sam. Sam Smith. Whenever Kenny was away and going to be gone for a couple of hours, Sam's scooter was tucked round the hedge by your back door. There!'

'Right,' said the inspector. 'I'll come and take a formal statement from you this evening. Be at home. Now go. You, Mr Whetstone, see him out of sight. Miss Lightfoot, the best that I can offer you for the moment is the use of a dog towel, recently washed, followed by a lift home.'

'A dog towel will do very nicely, thank you,' Joan said. It seemed that the inspector, in addition to being a dog-lover and therefore by definition a good person, also had a heart of gold.

Ken returned from seeing Gerry on his way. 'It looks very much like my wife's bicycle. Does it have a rusty scrape on the left fork?'

It did.

Sixteen

Another day seemed to be vanishing into the limbo of time but the day's work had all been disposed of. On the road home in Inspector Laird's car, Joan had managed to explain, quite convincingly she thought, that she had never met the deceased lady, that she knew nothing about the circumstances of her disappearance and that her only knowledge about the deceased lady's amours had been Gerry's disclosure a few minutes earlier. This seemed to be accepted.

Joan's first act on reaching home had been to shower and change, just managing to beat Ken to use of the small bathroom. It was illogical, she knew, in an assistant keeper, but the idea of insect larvae crawling around her secret parts made her skin crawl. She was quite inured to the adult insects, she did not even flap at a wasp, but she was almost totally ignorant about the lifestyle of larvae like that of the dragonfly and they looked so ferocious that she had never become reconciled to them.

Ken was complaining that he was hungry again. Their afternoon tea had turned into a high tea but that had been some time ago and she could not grudge him a supper. While preparing her trout for the purpose, Joan fed the two dogs. Ken moved some of the old and surplus chairs into the garden. She and Ken sat down to the meal, pleasantly weary but clean and refreshed. 'Take all you want,' she told Ken. 'I haven't had time to make a sweet so there's just fruit and cheese. Tell me, can you see Sam Smith as your wife's lover ... and killer?'

Ken was indeed hungry. He had just filled his mouth and it took him some seconds to empty enough for polite speech. 'That's hardly a question for me,' he said at last. 'You're a woman. Does he have the sex appeal to make an acceptable lover?' Having cleverly posed a question that would require a lengthy answer, he concentrated again on his trout.

Joan took the question seriously. 'He's no beauty,' she said, 'but he has a certain charm. He's stocky and muscular. He's young and he has some of the appeal of the little boy lost. He has a nice smile when he cares to use it, but too often he tries to look as if he's been everywhere and done everything. His teeth are good. He looks after himself, keeps himself well shaved and clean – except for his nails and you really can't expect a farm worker to stay manicured. He's brash but I think he's probably shy beneath it. So I think yes, he could make himself attractive to women, especially a woman who was looking for it. As to whether he would kill ... I don't know. What do you think?'

Having demolished his share of the trout, Ken was ready to talk. 'Almost anybody could kill, if pushed far enough. There are exceptions, but he isn't one of them – I've seen him killing rats. He didn't enjoy it but it didn't bother him either. He doesn't seem to have much of a temper. He takes a lot of needling from old Gerry and he just laughs. Once, somebody's terrier took a nip at his leg and he only rubbed the place and got back to work.'

'He would know, if anybody did, how to work the machine,' Joan said.

'Anybody who'd ever seen it working could puzzle out the controls in ten minutes, even by moonlight. The syndicate members have all been shown.'

'Most women couldn't,' Joan said thoughtfully. 'The feminists would go to the stake denying it, but we don't exactly shine with mechanical things. We leave that to men. But there's not a lot of doubt that we're looking for a man. You can think up – what do you call them? – scenarios in which she's killed by an angry wife defending her marriage, but they don't carry conviction. Is Sam Smith a randy young stud? That's the crunch question.'

Ken paused in the act of peeling an apple. 'You hardly ever see him out of an evening with a girl on his arm, but who knows what that means? You're more likely to come across him on a pub crawl with some mates. I've never heard any complaints about him from fond mothers.'

Ken was interrupted by a knock at the front door. Joan was in the act of applying Cheddar to a water biscuit, so Ken went to answer it. He came back with Sam Smith.

'Sit down,' Joan said. Sam stood, hesitating. 'Sit down,' Joan repeated more vehemently, 'or buzz off. I'm not having you tower over me in my own home.'

Sam lowered himself reluctantly into a chair. Joan poured him a mug of tea. 'What did you come to say?'

'You know, don't you?'

Joan and Ken did not go so far as to share a look. Each was no more than conscious of the other seen in the corner of the eye, yet they arrived at a common decision. Sam was not going to be given the easy option. He was going to have to spell it out. 'Know what?' Ken asked him.

Sam's usually bland face showed a trace of anger. 'You know bloody well. It didn't happen often, maybe six or seven times, but the first time she'd already made it plain that I wouldn't be unwelcome if I called in while you were away. I won't wrap it up with words like love – there was no love in it, just bloody good sex. The old mating. She was a lovely ride – whether you mind me saying so or not – and if I'd been you I'd've clung on to her, but I'm not and you didn't and if a woman like that was going round begging for it I don't see why I shouldn't have had my share.'

'Nor do I,' Ken said mildly. 'You don't have to sound so defiant about it. Why did you start off by saying that I knew? Knew what? That you'd been having sex with my late wife?'

'Yes. The sergeant-woman came to my door just now, to tell me that the inspector wants to see me first thing in the morning. And then, as she turned away, she winked at me.' Sam's face, which was tanned by exposure to the weather, did not show a blush but he sounded as though he might be blushing. He was looking at Ken. 'You'd just got out of the inspector's car. I can put two and two together. You know about me and your missus. Now they've left me to worry about it overnight.'

'So you came rushing round here,' Joan said, 'just to make sure that the police knew that you were worried about it.'

If Sam had been blushing, Joan's words quenched it. His face blanched under the tan. 'No. I wanted to get it over. And I ... I came partly to say I was sorry, though she swore that you never knew. It had finished before she went off. I know I shouldn't ... She was such a ... a magical woman and I don't have much success with girls. I don't have an education like you or many prospects so by the time ... '

'It's all right,' Ken said. 'You weren't the only one.'

'Yes, but what I really came to say was to ask you not to tell the police. Bloody silly thing to say, when *they* already as good as told *me*. You think it was a trap?'

'What do *you* think?' Joan asked.

'I think it was a trap and I've walked into it. Well, the harm's done and at least we can talk about it now.' He paused. Joan noticed that his fingers were shaking. 'I don't think she meant a lot to you?' Ken shook his head. 'I'd been hoping I hadn't hurt you. But I hope you can understand. She was such a totally feminine woman that when she offered herself to me I couldn't have helped myself even if I'd wanted to. Which I didn't, to be honest. You probably know this better than I do, but she had the knack.' He paused and looked at Joan. 'You don't have to listen to this.'

'I'm learning all the time,' Joan said. 'What knack?'

'The knack of ... I don't know how to put it, but those girls in the strip clubs don't come close to her. I knew that I was no more to her than somebody to pass the time with until somebody better came along. I didn't care. I didn't even like her very much. When she broke it off I knew I'd miss the fun of it but I wouldn't miss *her*. I still don't. And what I most wanted to say was that I never laid a finger on her.' He pulled a face. 'And that's another bloody silly thing to say, isn't it? We know I laid a lot more than that ... But

I never hurt her. I wouldn't have killed her.

'On that last day, the Friday, I was on my scooter and coming back towards the big house. There was two or three women standing blethering, not far from the silage tower. Your missus had been standing talking to Mr Watson but she walked on. As I came level, she waved me down. She asked for a lift home on my pillion, perfectly friendly, and I said yes. She hopped on and I dropped her at your gate. I only went to collect my pay packet and then I rode back past those wifies, so they must know that we were still on friendly terms but no more'n that.'

'No bicycle just then?' Joan asked.

Sam frowned. 'No, no bicycle. Funny, that.'

'You went off too,' Ken said, 'just after my wife left.'

'Hey! You didn't think I went to join her?'

Ken tried to not show that he was amused. 'No. I never thought that. But you went and you came back. Why was that?'

'Simple enough,' Sam said. 'A mate of mine came into his dad's farm. He knew about money but he knew damn-all about farming. His idea was that I'd look to the crops and the beasts and he'd attend to the finances and the ministry's paperwork. It worked fine for a while, but then he began to think he knew about farming. He wanted to make the decisions. They were decisions that maybe looked good on paper but they didn't *work*. Added to that, my mum was ill. So I packed it in and came back here.' He drained his mug of tea, which must by then have been cold, and got to his feet. 'I'm glad we've spoken,' he said.

'So am I,' Ken said when Joan returned from seeing Sam Smith on his way. 'Glad that we spoke, I mean. But we should have asked him who the wives were, the ones who saw him give my wife a lift. They'd go a long way towards suggesting his innocence.'

'If you can see that, so can he,' said Joan. 'He will almost certainly tell the police all about it. If he doesn't, we'll know. If he does we'll soon know whether they believe or disbelieve him. In other words, we can do no more about young Sam but his credibility or lack of it will soon be evident to all. But I don't believe that he's guilty. If he'd killed your wife and hidden her body in a straw bale, would he ever have come back here?'

'You've heard about murderers returning to the scene of the crime?' said Ken.

'I have. But I've never believed it. Or I'll put it another way. A murderer can't afford to draw attention to himself. That means that he must stick to the same routine. That's the only reason he'd return to the scene. Can you identify any of her other lovers?'

Ken shrugged. 'Damned if I can. She didn't exactly give out receipts or keep a list of phone— *Oh my God!*'

'What is it?'

'My subconscious has been working but it's only just got there. He said Friday afternoon, didn't he? The police will have picked up on that; or if they haven't, they will. So it was Friday afternoon she met Mr Watson. But my dinner and talk with the Deputy Assistant Chief Constable was at and after the conference dinner on the Saturday. I left to go to the conference on the Friday afternoon. I registered, had a snack meal and spent the evening going over the conference papers but I could easily have driven back here, done the deed and driven back again. As a matter of fact, I didn't sleep too well in a strange bed and without my usual ration of fresh air and walking, so I must have yawned off and on, that morning. You see what this means?'

'Yes. It means that you don't have your alibi any more. It also means that we'd better help the police to catch the real killer quickly, before they get fixated on you for the culprit. Don't you know any of her cleaning employers? Tentatively, we're looking for somebody male, footloose or in an unhappy marriage, well heeled and randy, with too much of a stake locally to abandon it and flee abroad.'

Ken looked at the ceiling while he thought. 'I can think of one or two who fit that description but as far as I know she never met any of them. Except possibly ... '

'Yes? Who?'

'What about your friend Tasker O'Neill?'

Joan's eyebrows shot up. 'He's rich all right, single and he acts randy although the spirit is more willing than the flesh. But I'd be surprised if he ever met her.'

'I'd be surprised if he hadn't,' Ken said. He pushed his mug forward. 'Pour me some more tea and I'll tell you. It goes back to when I tried to teach him how to cast a fly, when he'd inherited the cottage. He was trying himself out in the role of country gentleman. She got a phone message through Mrs Charles, but from Mr Watson, to say that somebody would be staying in the cottage for a few days and would she clean the place and ... "help out", those were the words. It was my wife who arranged that I'd go and give him tuition. He never showed any talent or appreciation for country ways.'

Silence fell over the pair like a blanket. The concept was new and difficult to accept. 'It's going to be almost impossible to produce any evidence,' Joan said at last. 'I don't have keys to his flat any more. Her body's burned. The police might be able to find traces connecting the two, but I wouldn't give much for their chances – not enough, anyway, to be worth drawing attention to my relationship with him.'

Ken put down his empty mug and pushed it forward for another refill. A long day without much fluid and an overproduction of adrenaline had dried his mouth. 'You're right,' he said. 'No need to make any rash decisions until we hear what the police have to say to me and to Sam tomorrow. After that, we'll have a better idea of which way things are going. We'll sleep on it.' He stretched until she heard his joints crack. 'Damn! I wanted to get into Newton Lauder tomorrow morning and deposit the money we got as tips before it gets lost or pinched.'

'I could do that for you,' Joan said. 'At the

same time, I could deposit what little's left of the money I gathered up on my overnight foray. It's time that that was laundered.' She got up and fetched her tea caddy. She began to count the notes. A slip of white paper fell from between them. 'Sixty-five,' she said.

'What's that?'

'Sixty-five.'

Ken shook his head impatiently. 'That piece of paper.'

'Just junk. I'll throw it away.'

'No.' Ken made a grab and flattened out the small page. It had both printing and writing on it. 'You don't know what this is. It's the receipt I was looking for. The one I wanted for my tax return. The one that was in her pocket when she went off.' Joan put out a hand to pick it up but he caught her wrist. 'Let's not add any more fingerprints,' he said. 'She was meticulous, I'll say that for her. She didn't touch what little money I had in the house but she took what she'd saved from her earnings. I suppose that whoever killed her saw no sense in abandoning the money—'

'Or thought that it might be traceable to him?'

'Or just that. So he took it. Where did you get it from?'

Joan thought back over the months. 'I was careful to take just one or two notes from each purse or pocket. Not enough to be missed. I'd have noticed an extra piece of paper. That was until the last house, Mr Farrow, the antiques dealer. I was in almost complete darkness and there was a fat wad of money in the wallet in his coat pocket. So I just grabbed some from the middle, about as thick as a pencil. Your receipt would have had to be in that lot.'

Seventeen

They sat up later than usual while they tried to digest the sudden gift that fate had thrown at them. When they retired to bed, sleep was slow to come. 'Of course,' Joan said at last, sleepily, 'he fits the criteria perfectly. Well-off bachelor, sexually demanding and with a strong local connection. But unless his fingerprints are on that receipt we've no physical evidence at all.'

Ken floated up near to the surface of sleep. 'Don' need physical,' he said. 'Give'm good pointer and they can fin' witnesses. Get 'm looking at someb'dy else. Now go sleep.'

Over breakfast he said, 'Are you going into the town, then, while I talk with the fuzz?'

'Yes. I want to bank that money and do some shopping. Our bank balance will be comparatively healthy for once. We want to make the most of each other, just in case, and I want to be nice for you.'

He looked at her in surprise, suddenly moved by her devotion and by the thought that they might become separated by the cumbersome proceedings of the law. 'You're always nice for me,' he said. 'If I'm reading you right, you're worried because you don't wrap yourself in girly things and wear a lot of makeup and perfume and high heels. But my wife did all that and where is she now? You're quite tall enough and your legs go on and on. And the smell of your soap is quite enough perfume. I see you and ... and love you as a hard-working partner. Then, when we're just ourselves, you're all the girl I want. If you want to make yourself nicer for me, that's fine, but you're only giving your confidence a boost it shouldn't need, because I've had a bellyful of feminine lures. Just go on being you and I'll be contented.

More than contented. Delighted.'

Joan looked at him although he was going a little misty around the edges. 'Thank you. That's just what I wanted to hear.'

Ken cleared his throat noisily. 'I've been thinking. I think you should go and see my pal Keith Calder. I told you about him. He owns the gun shop in the Square. He has a sort of connection with the police, because his daughter married the local detective inspector, but I'm told that he also does private detective work. He can usually get at the truth and he can hold his tongue. Go and tell him the story in confidence and ask for his advice.'

'That's putting an awful lot of trust in a stranger, isn't it?'

'Yes. But I can't think of anyone else to turn to. I trust him.'

'I trust both you and your judgement. Will he want a fee up front?'

'I don't suppose so. I hope not.'

'Just in case, I'll call on him before I go to the bank.' She got up and went to the cupboard. The tea caddy was on a different shelf from the usual but her money was intact. Her attention was drawn to a vase that was tucked away behind a ginger jar. It started a small bell ringing. She pulled out the vase.

'Where did this come from? I haven't seen it before. Or have I?'

He laughed. 'There's a bit of a story there, a series of coincidences. It belonged to somebody my wife used to clean for. I don't know who, so don't bother asking. She broke it one day while the owner was out and came home in a tizzy because the owner was somebody she didn't want to fall out with. It wasn't very valuable – a cheap Japanese copy of a Chinese original and it happened that we had a very similar one. My wife spotted it in a junk shop one day and was sure that it was a valuable piece of Ming. The fact that she was allowed to buy it for about ten pee should have told her that it wasn't. So she took it away with her while I tried to repair the broken one. I couldn't make a very good job of it and now I don't know who it belonged to.' He suddenly tensed. 'You mean that if we could trace its owner we could find one of her clients? We'd have to search through a whole lot of houses.'

Once she was on her feet, Joan had begun the washing-up. She turned and leaned back against the sink. The vase was in her hands. He was right, he had not made a very good job of the repair. 'But I know who the owner is,' she said. 'At least, I've seen one that looked identical.' It took her a few seconds of frantic mental activity to drag recollection to the surface. Then, suddenly, it fitted together. 'It was in the house of Farrow, the antiques dealer, the man whose money had the receipt in, the one you wanted—'

Ken was roused but he still managed to chuckle. 'No need to go on like "The House that Jack Built",' he said. 'It would seem that Farrow was among my wife's lovers.'

'And that he killed her,' Joan said firmly. 'The vase would be one that came among a lot of better china and he used it to fill a gap at home rather than try to resell rubbish.'

'That's making a leap in the dark. You could be right, but we can't go rushing to the police and say, "Look how innocent we are, here's the real villain." Not without revealing you as the master criminal that you are.'

Joan gave him a rap on the head with her knuckles, but it was a friendly rap. Her mind had raced ahead but it had come up against the apparently insuperable obstacle that they could not take her knowledge to the police without revealing her as a burglar. 'I'll see your Mr Calder straight away. It's a desperate resort, but if we try to handle this without outside advice we're going to blow it.'

'I'll phone and tell him that you'll be coming.'

An overnight frost had pushed the landscape further in the direction of autumn, but the day was bright and pretending to be warm. Joan enjoyed the golden colours of the trees and stubbles. The blaze of Virginia creeper on a gable raised her spirits a little. She wished she could have been in the fresh air on the scooter rather than cooped up in the Land Rover's noisy, fume-laden cab. Perhaps, if the tips kept flowing and she took on some domestic jobs around the estate and the town, she could send the motorcycle shop a cheque and keep the scooter. But perhaps not. Better perhaps to cut the connection and buy another one. Her brief custody of the scooter had given her a taste for personal transport.

She found an unoccupied parking slot in the Square almost opposite the dignified frontage of the gun shop, but before she could even stop the engine a man opened the passenger door and got in beside her. 'Drive,' he said.

The abrupt greeting surprised her but she

replied in similar vein. 'Drive where?'

'Anywhere. Somewhere that we won't be disturbed. Ken phoned me. We may want to be private. We may even not want it known that we've spoken.'

'All right. You direct me.'

Following his directions, she drove out of the town to the north and then took to a ride through an area of mixed woodland and forestry plantation. When the road was out of sight, they parked.

'Now,' he said, 'tell me the whole story.'

She would have put his age at around sixty although the agility with which he had entered the Land Rover suggested that he was very fit. His face was little lined except by laughter-lines. He was good looking in a Spanish or Italian manner and Joan guessed that earlier he would have been classed definitely as handsome. He was dressed for the country, but his suede golf jacket would, she thought, have looked very well on Ken.

If Ken said that he could be trusted then she would trust him. She began at the beginning, making no attempt to whitewash herself. She held his eyes so that she could tell when he was amused or sympathetic. If he had disbelieved her she would have known, so she was frank, beginning with the nature of her background, her attempts at self-education and her escape from home to Edinburgh. The use of a bottle to subdue a violent approach he accepted as understandable. Her months under the protection of Tasker O'Neill produced no reaction and she guessed that he had enjoyed a few such relationships in the past.

He listened with intense concentration and asked a few questions as she dealt with the matter of the earrings and the death of Mr Jenkins; but as she followed on with the theft of the scooter, her acquisition of Dram and her burglarious raid on some of the houses of Newton Lauder, he was clearly amused. She spoke frankly of her affair with Ken and of the earlier disappearance of his wife. Although the police had been very reticent with the press, garbled word of the finding of the burned body was circulating in the town; but Keith Calder, by virtue of his connections in the police, seemed to know more than was generally available.

She came at last to the reasons why she and Ken were so concerned. She dragged her mind away from emotion and tried to stay strictly with the facts. 'The police are interviewing Ken now,' she said. 'He's wide open to be suspected of killing his wife. And my position is worse because I can be suspected of complicity in the death of Mr Jenkins and I am actually guilty of robbing several houses. We can be almost sure that we know who killed Ken's wife but we can't tell it to the police unless I own up to being the phantom burglar of Newton Lauder. And after that they'll have me charged as an accomplice to the murder of Mr Jenkins.'

'There's no such charge as complicity in Scotland,' he said. He gave a short chuckle. 'I knew that we'd be having some such discussion ever since I first saw you in the Square. You were blonde. A day or two later you were raven-haired. A brunette will often bleach herself but outside the theatrical profession it's almost unheard of for a blonde to go dark.' He sat in silence for a minute or more. Once he laughed again and then looked serious. She waited patiently. At last, he stirred. 'But we'd better try to get the jeweller's murder out of the way. Do you keep up with the Scottish news?'

She looked at him in surprise. 'Not really. You can't get the papers delivered but one of us sometimes brings one home. We don't have a radio in the Land Rover. We usually catch the national news summary and leave it at that.'

Keith Calder produced a mobile phone, scrolled through the listed names and settled on one. 'This is a journalist who owes me favours,' he said. 'He does court reporting for the *Evening News.* If anyone knows, he ... Hullo? Kenny?'

For several minutes Joan was subjected to the infuriating experience of hearing one side of a conversation. Whenever she thought that she understood, the next words disabused her. In the end, however, Keith Calder ended the call.

'I've known young Honeypot for a few years,' he said. 'She used to be based here. She comes over as a very open and friendly person, but she can be very devious. I think she knew damn well who you were and she was holding her hand because she could squeeze you and Ken for everything you know while you're feeling vulnerable.'

'Are you saying that I don't have to feel vulnerable?'

'About the death of Mr Jenkins, no, you don't. We'll try to sort out your other misdeeds as we go along.

'I'll tell you what happened in the case of Mr Jenkins. You referred to the man as a gentleman and it turns out that that's what he was, as well as being a criminal and a murderer. He seems to have stabbed Mr Jenkins in an act of panic and he left his knife behind with his fingerprints on it. He was also picked out of a line-up by witness after witness. His lawyer advised him to enter a guilty plea and then make all the arguments about no previous convictions, sudden panic, bitter regret and so on and so forth. That's exactly what he did and then immediately added a statement that you were an innocent dupe, that he'd never seen you before and he involved you on the spur of the moment. He got away with a sentence that was remarkably lenient in the circumstances.

'The police accepted his statement about you after making enquiries; and I understand that those enquiries were made by Honeypot herself, so that it didn't take her long to connect you with the vanished Celia Lightfoot. She probably intends to break the good news to you as soon as you've either told all you know or tangled yourself in a web of lies.'

'And I was quite prepared to like her,' Joan said indignantly. 'I think she's a nasty – what was the word you used? Devious, that was it. I think she's a devious bitch and if I get the chance to drop her in it, in she goes. But first we have to get Ken and me out of it. Can you help us? In fact, knowing what I've told you, are you willing to help us?'

He laughed once more. 'You seem to be hinting that I might leave you in the lurch because circumstances drove you to commit a little burglary in order to support a dependent spaniel. I love your emulation of Flannelfoot and your idea, more resembling Robin Hood, of only taking a small sum from each. As for Mr James Farrow, I noticed some time ago how roughly he treated his spaniel and had thought of doing something similar myself; and if a few hundred quid came along with the deal, so much the better. Killing an importunate lover I would not put beyond him and if he's guilty he can suffer for it. This isn't my usual line – I usually investigate gun crime on behalf of the defence – but I think I can see ways and means.'

Joan felt a lightening of the burden. 'Then you must be cleverer than I am,' she said.

'You said it first, I didn't. In one area, you need to depart from the truth. When you do that, you have to be absolutely sure that there are no contradictions that you can't explain and you, or both, or all, must be agreed and determined to stick to the whole story like glue, through thick and thin and in the teeth of cross-examination by experts. Can you do that? Think about it.'

She thought about it. She also put Ken into her place. Confronted with the certainty of separation, probably for years, she was confident. 'I think I can speak for myself and for Ken,' she said. 'Tell me the tale we have to tell and I'll be more definite.'

His eyes had developed a new twinkle and he had a mischievous smile. She realized suddenly that he was enjoying himself. 'It all hinges on that receipt and how and when it came into your hands. On the face of what you've told me, the only significant fingerprints on it should be yours, Ken's and James Farrow's and nobody can say when it came into your possession except possibly Mr Farrow if he ever realized that his working capital had suddenly diminished.'

'I don't understand ... '

'Of course you don't. Listen carefully and I'll explain.' He spoke on, softly, for some minutes. Joan listened, fascinated, as Keith spelled out her options in various contingencies. By the time he'd finished, he had her laughing. He put his hand on the door.

'I'll run you back to your shop,' she said.

He smiled his very charming smile. 'No

need.' He pointed to the peak of a gable showing above the trees. 'That's my house there.'

Eighteen

When Joan parked in the Square in Newton Lauder, her mind was seething with thoughts, each trying to override the others for a place in her plan. The first to triumph was that returning home too early might be a mistake. She had no wish to meet the police before conferring with Ken. Even use of the telephone might arouse suspicions if she happened to catch him closeted with the detective inspector. She span out her visit to the bank, treated herself to coffee and then dawdled around the shop windows.

Driven by curiosity and a total lack of anything else to do, she set off at last and approached the heart of the estate by way of the western drive. She made her approach cautiously, turning off before the farm buildings came in sight and making her way up a track which was muddy in almost all weathers. The track ended at a triangle of rough ground beside a small wood that held the largest of the release pens. Leaving the Land Rover, she only had to walk a few yards and she gained the view that she wanted. The scorched area where the fire had burned was conspicuous in the stubble-field although all the debris had been meticulously removed for laboratory study. The field was criss-crossed by tapes and a fingertip search was continuing in one of the remoter squares but without any great enthusiasm or expectation being evident.

At the keeper's cottage there was no sign of a police presence and while she watched, a figure recognizable as that of Ken emerged into the back garden and began to dig, which was Ken's habit when perturbed or at a loose end. So far only the first few yards adjacent to the cottage had been brought under cultivation, which said something for Ken's peace of mind and lack of leisure. The two dogs were with him – Mr Watson must be away at his constituency office – and they sat down to watch. Even at a distance, the labrador was clearly visible as a black dot. The spaniel's camouflage made it more difficult to pick out but wherever Ken and Dram were, there would Tanya be also.

She checked the traps and the feed supply, in case anybody should ask the reason for her side-trip, before returning to the Land Rover and shooing away the few pheasants that had decided to take advantage of the warmth of the bonnet. She bounced and skidded back down the hill and parked in front of the cottage. She heard the dogs bark once to acknowledge her return and when Ken opened the back door they hurried inside to welcome her home. By then, she had the kettle on and her coat off.

Ken had to remove his gardening boots. He was lightly dusted with loam. He kissed Joan as a matter of course and took a seat in the kitchen. Joan was putting out the coffee mugs. 'He doesn't want a fee,' she said. 'Did you know that he runs the shoot next door? It used to be the Hay estate before I went to Edinburgh but it belongs to Mrs Ilwand now.'

'I thought I told you that much.'

'If you did, I'd forgotten. All he wants in the way of a fee is for us to lamp for foxes on Long Barrow, which we were doing anyway.'

'No problem,' Ken said. 'Now, was he any help?'

Joan poured hot water on the coffee granules. 'Brilliant. But first, what did you tell the police?'

'The absolute truth about myself, my movements and my relationship with my wife. About you, I only said that you turned up, staying in the Loch Cottage, and knew the keepering job, so I took you on as my assistant and the relationship grew.'

'That's good. Did you tell them about the receipt?'

Ken shook his head. 'I didn't know how that would fit in with whatever you were going to tell them.'

As he spoke, Joan heard the sound of tyres outside and the ratchet of a parking brake. 'Here they come,' she said urgently. 'Your pal suggested that the receipt arrived among the tips. I only found it this morning. Follow my lead.'

She folded the receipt into an empty envelope and left the kitchen in response to a peremptory rapping at the front door. The Range Rover was nose to nose with the Land Rover and making the latter look very workaday. Detective Sergeant Lindsay was on the doorstep with Detective Inspector Laird beside her. Both were smiling.

'May we come in?' asked the sergeant.

'Please do,' Joan said. She spoke up in case her words should be drowned by the sound of the butterflies in her stomach. She led the way into the hall.

'Perhaps we could see Mr Whetstone at the same time,' Inspector Laird suggested.

'I was going to suggest the same thing,' Ken said from the kitchen door.

Within a few seconds, the group was seated in the small sitting room. The visitors refused coffee but Joan went for the unfinished mugs. Her mouth was dry and no representatives of the police, even smiling female ones, were going to deprive her of her coffee. The sergeant opened the customary notebook on her knee but also placed a small tape recorder on the coffee table from the Loch Cottage. Joan and Ken shared the big settee and surreptitiously, as they thought, linked hands.

'Let's begin by going over again what you already told us, Mr Whetstone,' said Honeypot. 'Have you remembered any of the households that your wife went to on her housekeeping duties?'

'I already explained,' Ken said, 'that I very rarely knew any of them. She never asked me for transport. Usually she cycled to wherever she was going. I know that she went once or twice to the Loch Cottage and she helped out at the big house occasionally.

That's all.'

'I see. Tell me again when you last saw your wife, just to be sure that we've got it straight.'

'I saw her at lunchtime on that Friday. She said nothing about going out. I told her that I would be leaving for my weekend course soon after and I did so. I expected her to be at home when I returned late on the Sunday, but she had gone and I never saw her – alive – again.'

'Thank you. Miss Lightfoot, where were you staying before you came here?'

Joan blessed the inspiration that had caused Ken to send her to Keith Calder. She spoke clearly for the benefit of the tape recorder. 'I think you know very well, Inspector. You were the investigating officer who cleared me of any involvement in the death of Mr Jenkins. I had left Edinburgh by then because I did not know that the real killer was going to make a statement that would clear me. Did you intend to set my mind at rest?'

Clearly Inspector 'Honeypot' Laird was caught on the wrong foot. She turned again to Ken. 'Nor did you know the identity of your wife's lover?'

'Or lovers,' Ken said. 'I neither knew nor

cared. We had lost interest in each other. I assume that he was somebody she had met through her cooking and cleaning visits.'

Joan thought that this was the point at which the inspector had intended to put pressure on Ken through her. With Joan aware that she had been exonerated of any part in the death of Mr Jenkins, the interrogation had rather lost its head of steam. 'Surely,' said the inspector, 'she must have encountered some other men.'

'Shopkeepers,' Ken said. 'But she could never have expected one of them to run away with her. Sometimes she helped out at the big house and served lunch when the syndicate was shooting here.'

'I find your choice of words interesting. Why would you suppose that your wife expected her lover to run away with her?'

Ken was not perturbed by what was intended as a trick question. The inspector was grasping at straws. 'Surely it's obvious?' he said. 'There could be a hundred reasons for a man to kill a woman, but in this instance the most likely scenario is that she wanted to be rescued from an unhappy marriage, a small cottage and a life of work far from what she had come to regard as civilization. She put pressure on a man who had his own reasons not to play along with her. Perhaps he is well established here with a lifestyle that he wouldn't want to leave behind. Perhaps he has other amorous irons in the fire.'

Inspector Honeypot was still looking at him keenly. 'And which of the local men would you say was most likely to fill that role?'

Joan could see them circling endlessly around the point. 'To cut out a whole lot of speculative debate,' she said, 'may I say something?'

'Of course, Miss Lightfoot.' Honeypot's smile had faded considerably but it made a sudden return. 'Or may I call you Joan?'

'Of course. If I can call you Honeypot.'

The smile vanished again. 'Go on.'

'I went to the bank this morning to pay in most of the money we received in tips at last Saturday's shoot. You understand the system?'

'I am well aware of the system, Miss Lightfoot. It is quite usual for the estate to be relieved of most of the wages of keepering and the VAT on those wages and on the fees paid by visitors, by requiring guest Guns to tip not less than a substantial minimum. You would have had quite a large sum to pay in.'

'Yes,' said Joan, 'I did. And I found between the notes a receipt that Ken had been in need of. He had complained to me, more than once, that his wife had gone off with it in her pocket. We will give you our fingerprints for purposes of comparison. You may find the guilty party's fingerprints are also on it. At any rate, it strongly suggests that he was on Mr Watson's guest list.'

Inspector Laird fixed Joan with a penetrating stare. 'We will, of course, thoroughly investigate that suggestion. I sincerely hope that you are not attempting to throw dust in our eyes. For a start, I hardly think that any of Mr Watson's guests would be familiar with the working of the modern baler.'

'You're wrong,' Ken said bluntly. 'The farmers used to contract out the baling of straw and silage, but the machines were always busy just when they wanted them. So last year the estate purchased a baler and the biggest of the farmers, Jack Egglestone, was so tickled with it when it arrived that he showed it off to anyone interested who was around, which at the time happened to be the syndicate members on a working party. The function of the baler – picking up a big bale and manipulating it so that it wraps itself in polythene off the big roll – proved just as fascinating to the syndicate members and he gave anyone interested a practical lesson in operating it.'

Ken and the inspector fell silent, each busy with thoughts. Joan decided that the moment might be ripe for her to put in her oar again. 'There's another pointer to a syndicate member or one of the beating team. At the beaters' lunch I suggested that we might start the next shoot by walking the verges of the drive, because her bicycle had never been accounted for and it seemed likely that it had been dropped in the bracken. And almost immediately I find a lady's bicycle in the loch.'

The inspector was frowning. 'Surely that suggests one of the beaters rather than a Gun.'

'Not really. There's been a lot of interest in Mrs Whetstone's death and in the relationship between Ken and myself. Many of the Guns and beaters know each other. It was bound to be mentioned.'

'Which ones—?'

'Wait a minute,' Joan said. 'Before you waste your time and energy on a process of elimination that may go on for ever, may I offer you one more short cut?'

'Go ahead,' said the inspector.

'I quite appreciate that for the moment you have nobody's word for any of it but ours. However, there is another way to confirm the identity of at least one of Mrs Whetstone's employers. And that might start a chain reaction, one of them having recommended her to the next and so on. Ken, tell the Inspector about the Chinese pot. The one you showed me.'

'Japanese,' Ken corrected. 'A vase. And comparatively recent. Inspector, my wife came home one day, very upset because she had broken a vase in an employer's house. More upset, I may say, than the calamity was worth unless the owner was more to her than a mere employer, but perhaps I'm being wise in hindsight. She had brought the pieces back with her. It was an inexpensive piece, mass-produced in Japan in the Chinese style for the European market, but she thought that it was valuable.

'As it happened, we had an almost identical vase. My wife had bought it in a car-boot sale and deluded herself that it was of great antiquity and value. I fetched it for her to put back in place of the other before the owner returned. I tried to glue the original vase together again but it's not a very neat job. Some fingerprints may have survived. In any case, if you find a house with a similar vase in it, you'll have a strong indication; and if the owner's a syndicate member and his fingerprints are also on the receipt, I suggest that you'll have grounds for a thorough investigation of that man.'

Joan, knowing the story of the vase, had let her mind wander and was considering the various actions that the murderer must have taken. Any traces left by most of those actions would have been erased by time and by the fire, but ... 'One more moment,' she said. 'Apart from hypothetical fingerprints, what we've talked about were only indicators of people having been employers of Ken's late wife. But the man who killed her took her bike to the loch. He wouldn't have ridden it cross-country. If he had a quiet car he'd have driven into the west drive, found the bike, put it into his car and driven the long way round, to arrive at the loch just as you did, Inspector. Any ordinary car, even a four-by-four, would collect weeds and heather on the underneath. If he denies having been to the loch but you find matching traces, then he's in the position of having lied to the police.'

'None of the other syndicate members have been down to the loch?'

'Only Tasker O'Neill, and he came in the laird's Range Rover.'

'We'll be back in due course with statements for your signature,' the inspector said. The two officers got up and moved to the door. There was a new urgency in their movements.

'Hold on, ladies,' Ken said. 'You're forgetting your tape recorder.'

Nineteen

After Ken and Joan had signed their formal statements, contact with the police was suddenly reduced to occasional formalities. They were left to gather from this non-event and from word filtering back through the local grapevine as to what questions were being asked and places examined, that they were well off the suspect list.

The shop of J. D. Farrow, further along the street from that of Keith Calder (Gunmaker to very minor Royalty) and well beyond the Square, remained closed, but this was not unusual. When he was without a skilled assistant (as, being very short-tempered, was frequently the case) the shop was usually closed while he was away on a buying trip. This time, however, it remained shut until it was suddenly announced in the media that Mr Farrow had been charged with the year-old murder of Mrs Whetstone. He was not granted bail. The shop remained closed but was soon purchased as a going concern by an antiques dealer from Edinburgh whose lease had been bought out from under him.

Joan and Ken had a successful season. Some habitat improvements and an extra release pen enabled them to plan the release of an increased number of birds. This in turn would permit two extra let days, bringing the shoot closer to financial viability. It became possible to reduce the subscription required from syndicate members, which proved popular at the AGM. At the same time, the level of tips was increased. An attempt by the laird to gain an extra day for his own guests fell by the wayside when the secretary pointed out the extra financial input that would be required from him.

In general, the couple proved popular. With no doubt remaining that Ken was now a widower, they announced their engagement. At a confidential meeting, the syndicate members decided on a levy to contribute to the cost of the wedding, subject only to a mass invitation to attend it.

Joan's hair was recovering from a serious clipping. Ken had been conscripted into carrying out the deed, which he considered to be rank vandalism. For months she had worn a woollen hat. Now she could be seen to be her natural blonde self, but it would be another year before her hair returned to its earlier length.

The trial of Mr Farrow was called for early summer, shortly after the release of the new season's pheasant poults. No time is ideal for a keeper but this was perhaps as convenient as any. In return for some help with a sudden infestation of gapeworm, Keith Calder undertook to see that traps and snares were visited and the supply of grain and water was maintained.

The law customarily shrinks in horror from any idea that a court might have to take a recess because a witness was required ahead of the time for which he had been summoned. Thus Mr Watson (who was required to testify to his encounter with the late Mrs Whetstone), Joan (required in respect of the receipt) and Ken were all waiting in a dark and featureless witness room. Mr Watson had been promised that, in view of his supposed importance as a Member of Parliament, he would be dealt with early, and had then been forgotten.

Inspector 'Honeypot' Laird and Sergeant Lindsay, who were needed in the first instance to give evidence of arrest, should have been isolated in another, equally dismal, chamber. While the lawyers were engaged in a seemingly interminable wrangle over some procedural point of no importance whatever, they had wandered through to see that their essential witnesses were present, sane and sober.

After a few polite words about the weather Joan asked, 'How long will this case go on for?'

Inspector Laird shrugged. 'It needn't take long,' she said. She took a seat beside Joan. She was wearing a dress that looked, to Joan, remarkably like Versace. 'After being cautioned, he lost his temper and made some admissions in front of several witnesses and the video cameras. The lab exceeded itself and found both his fingerprints and his DNA on that receipt. But there are several young tigers out there keen to make their reputations and when a gaggle of lawyers get their teeth into a subject they can spin it out indefinitely.'

The ice being broken, Joan felt free to ask, 'When were you going to tell me that I had been cleared of Mr Jenkins's death?'

Honeypot smiled sweetly. 'When I was good and ready. If a witness is holding something back, it can help to keep them off balance.'

'Was I holding something back?' Joan asked.

'You still are. I don't know all of it and I don't want to know. This case is straightforward and I don't want it complicated by side issues.'

Joan sat up straight. 'You were playing dirty,' she said. 'I can understand that you might not let a guilty person know that you knew that he was guilty. But to let an innocent person think that she was still suspect, I don't think you were playing the game.'

Detective Inspector Honeypot was still smiling, but it was a smile of ice. She glanced at the door and then nodded to the sergeant who went and stood in the doorway. 'If we're talking about playing games,' the inspector said, 'what kind of games have you been playing? Would you happen to know anything about a motor scooter that disappeared from outside the dealer's shop in Edinburgh just before you came here and then just as mysteriously reappeared two days after I arrived?'

'Certainly not,' Joan said, but she could feel the heat as the blood rushed to her face.

Mr Watson, sensing that drama was imminent, muttered something and slipped away in the general direction of the toilets.

'And,' persisted Honeypot, 'you also would know nothing about a spaniel that disappeared from the heel of the accused and has never been seen again although its clone has been in your possession ever since that time?'

Joan was almost overcome by the sensation that the world was crumbling about her ears. She was prepared to face up to her guilt about the scooter, but to have Dram wrenched away from her would be beyond bearing. She managed to shake her head and utter a husky negative.

'But you seem to have acquired the spaniel within a week of leaving Edinburgh. You wouldn't care to explain?'

'I gave her the spaniel,' said Ken.

'And where did you get it from?'

'I bought it from a man in a pub,' Ken said.

There was a moment of shocked silence. Everyone present knew that he was lying.

'That's sweet,' said the sergeant. 'I like to see loyalty.'

'I was not going to pursue the matter anyway,' said Honeypot. 'When asked for an opinion of Mr Farrow as a person, almost everyone remarked on his cruelty towards the spaniel. In my book, that's worse than the charge he's facing. She's better in your hands.'

Detective Sergeant Lindsay had been their main, almost their only, channel of communication with the police during the past months and had turned out to be human and to have a well-developed sense of humour. She was still trying to emulate Honeypot's casual but expensive elegance but never quite succeeding. She was as curious as the next person. 'Tell me,' she said. 'When I first came to you and told you about the body in the ashes, you must have guessed that it was likely to be Mr Whetstone's wife. What was your first reaction? Joy or sorrow?'

Joan thought back and remembered that day. Her first frivolous thought returned to her. 'I thought of asking you to be a bridesmaid,' she said, laughing.

The sergeant was serious. She turned pink with pleasure. 'But that's lovely,' she said. 'Nobody ever asked me to be a bridesmaid before. I'd love to be a bridesmaid.'

Joan was horrified. She and Ken had been planning a simple knot tying before the registrar with the absolute minimum of family present. The sergeant's delighted acceptance was pushing them in the direction of a church and gowns and flowers and confetti.

Before she could find an acceptable form of words to withdraw what had seemed to be an invitation, they were interrupted. An usher appeared in the doorway. 'It's all over,' he said. 'The accused changed his plea. You can all go home.'

As they left the building, Detective Inspector 'Honeypot' Laird took hold of Joan's sleeve. 'You've had an adventurous time,' she said. 'Now stay firmly on the straight and narrow path. I'll be watching you.' (Joan opened her mouth to protest.) 'Look after the spaniel. And your husband,' she added as an afterthought.